The GIFT of the PIRATE QUEEN

PATRICIA REILLY GIFF

Illustrated by Jenny Rutherford

DELACORTE PRESS / NEW YORK

Published by
Delacorte Press
1 Dag Hammarskjold Plaza
New York, N.Y. 10017

Manufactured in the United States of America

First printing

Designed by Judith Neuman

Library of Congress Cataloging in Publication Data

Giff, Patricia Reilly.
The gift of the pirate queen.

Summary: Sixth-grader Grace, her mother dead and her
only sister ill with diabetes, learns to be brave like
the pirate queen Grace O'Malley, whom her Irish cousin
says she resembles.
[1. Irish-Americans—Fiction.   2. Death—Fiction.
3. Diabetes—Fiction]   I. Rutherford, Jenny, ill.
II. Title.
PZ7.G3626Gg   [Fic]   82-70310
ISBN 0-440-02970-8   AACR2
ISBN 0-440-02972-4 (lib. bdg.)

for my son
James Matthew Giff
with love

1

Grace was almost home, all the way to Mr. Hunt's field, before she remembered. "I have to go back for my social studies book," she told her sister, Amy. "We have punish work for the weekend."

"Again?" Amy pulled her hat down farther over her ears and shivered. "Want me to wait?"

Grace shook her head. "No. Go ahead." She crossed the dirt road at the end of the field and turned on to the town road. Then she started to run, counting the streets as she crossed them: Meredith, Front, Baxter, and Linter.

By the time she reached School Street and the Danville Valley School, she was out of breath. She slowed down as she went around to the school yard and pulled open the heavy side doors.

It was quiet in the hall. The only sounds were the

rubbery slap of her boots against the tile floor and the hum of the fluorescent light near the stairs.

She passed Amy's classroom and went back to peek through the little window in the door. Mrs. Gold, the fourth-grade teacher, was bent over her desk, marking papers.

Grace stood there for a moment. If only she had Mrs. Gold again, or Miss Patterson, her old fifth-grade teacher.

She turned the hall corner and went up the stairs to the second floor. The door to the sixth-grade room was open, but Mrs. Raphael was gone.

The room looked strange without anyone in it. The boards were erased and the desks were cleared. All except for Lisa Kile's, the new girl who had come in October. Surrounded by empty space, her desk had a little ball of crumpled paper and a ball-point pen on it.

Grace closed her eyes.

"Stop touching that pen," Mrs. Raphael had told Lisa this morning. Her mouth was thin and tight and stretched into a narrow line. "Sometimes I wonder why I spend my life trying to make all of you pay attention. In my other school . . ." She pressed the tip of her finger against her bottom lip and stared out the window. "In Warwick the children wanted to learn." She turned back to them. "I want to hear about the United Nations," she said suddenly.

The room became still. No one moved.

"Why was it founded? By whom?"

Grace clenched her hands together in her lap, trying to remember. She could picture the page in the book, the side it was on, even the paragraph. Who . . .

It was hard to think with Mrs. Raphael looking around the room, ready to pick on someone . . . someone she would question and question until the person finally had to give up. And then she'd smile a little. "See," she'd say, "I told you. You don't study."

Now Mrs. Raphael's eyes caught Lisa, two desks away from Grace. "Can you tell us, Lisa?"

Grace could feel everyone sit back, relieved that it was someone else, someone like Lisa Kile. All the girls called Lisa a cootie, and the boys said she was a retard. Each day the kids who sat near her inched their desks away until it looked as if Lisa were on an island all by herself.

Grace looked over at her. Lisa was staring at the blackboard, eyes half-closed. She probably hadn't even heard Mrs. Raphael calling on her. Grace watched as Lisa reached into her desk and tore a little piece of paper out of her assignment pad. She rolled it slowly between her fingers, then brought it up to her mouth. Still looking at the blackboard, she began to chew it.

"Lisa." Mrs. Raphael's voice was high, shrill.

Lisa jumped.

"Take that candy and . . ."

Lisa shook her head. Her hair was snarled, as if she had forgotten to comb it. "Don't have candy."

"Take that gum or whatever it is . . ."

Lisa reached into her mouth.

"And get out," Mrs. Raphael said. "Stand in the hall." She picked up her record book. "All of this is going down," she said. "All of it. Permanently." She took a pen off the desk and began to write.

In the back of the room someone whispered something. Mrs. Raphael looked up. "Since no one wants to get down to work, you can do the questions at the end of the chapter by yourselves. For homework."

Grace sighed and opened her eyes. Homework. She had come back to get her social studies book. She looked around at the empty classroom. In the gray December light Mrs. Raphael's desk was in shadows.

Grace went over to it and stared at the big gold letters in the record book. CLASS RECORDS. She reached out, then pulled her hand back. Somehow, she knew, Mrs. Raphael would know if she opened it. It was odd about Mrs. Raphael. The first time Grace had seen her, she'd thought she was beautiful. Her eyes were large and brown and her blond hair was curled softly around her face. But now Grace didn't think Mrs. Raphael was pretty at all. There were frown lines in her forehead and she never smiled.

Grace looked at the other things on the desk: the

big green blotter, the ink pad, a neat pile of pencils with sharp points, and the Christmas bell.

Mrs. Raphael had brought the bell in today. The bell and a little Christmas tree for the table in the corner of the room. "Decorations," she had said. "All from the children at my last school. From Warwick. Years ago." She had held the bell up for them to see. Caught in the sunlight for a moment, the bell shimmered, sending a pink rainbow across Mrs. Raphael's desk.

Grace leaned forward. Now, up close, she could see the bell more clearly. It was shaped like an angel. Its eyes were closed and the tiny glass hands were folded over a long pink skirt.

Without thinking, Grace reached out and gently touched one feathery wing. It seemed strange that Mrs. Raphael had the angel on her desk, strange that she owned anything so dainty and beautiful. Grace wondered if Mrs. Raphael had been different in the other school so that the children had loved her and wanted to give her something wonderful like the bell.

Carefully Grace picked it up, listening to the tinkling sound it made when she moved it.

Behind her, suddenly, the door slammed.

She twirled around.

The bell slipped out of her hands. It hit the edge of Mrs. Raphael's chair, and then the floor with a sharp, high sound.

For a moment she stared at the broken glass in horror. Then she looked back at the door. The wind. Just the wind. No one was there.

Heart pounding, she crouched down next to the desk. The bell lay there in pieces. Her hands were slippery wet, her mouth dry. "Please," she whispered, "please." She braced one hand against the desk, feeling that she couldn't catch her breath. Then she opened her eyes and reached out to touch the splintery sharp edges of the angel's skirt.

2

Grace ran down the stairs and out the heavy doors. She could almost feel the knobby weight of the angel pieces she had wrapped in looseleaf and tucked in her schoolbag.

She kept running even after she reached the end of the town road. Breathless, she took the shortcut across Mr. Hunt's field. Ralph, Mr. Hunt's goat, was standing at the edge of his pen, his beard poking through the holes in the chicken wire. She called to him but she didn't stop until she reached her own backyard and Willie's pen.

She tried to whistle at her goat, but her mouth was too dry. Instead she reached in between the wires and rubbed Willie's nose. Then slowly she went up the three wooden steps to the back porch.

For a moment she expected to see her mother through the kitchen window. She'd be standing at the stove, her long hair straight on her back, wearing an old pair of jeans and her red sweater. Grace could picture her turning, holding out her arms. But then, when she thought about looking up at her mother's face, she couldn't remember what she looked like. She couldn't remember her nose, or her eyes, or the shape of her mouth.

She banged the door open. Only Amy was there. Of course. Amy was sitting at the kitchen table, her dark hair long like her mother's. She had a piece of toast in her hand.

"Oh, Amy. I . . ." Grace began. She stopped when she saw the thin smear of jelly on Amy's cheek.

"What's the matter?" Amy asked.

"Never mind. Why are you eating that?"

"What?"

"Jelly."

Amy pushed the jar across the table. "Strawberry. Want some?"

"I hate it when you do that," Grace said.

"Push the jar . . . ?"

"No. Eat the jelly."

"I hate it when you start to get bossy," Amy said, "and nag like an old lady."

"If I had diabetes, I wouldn't need anyone to tell me—"

Amy took a bite of her toast. "A little sugar won't kill me."

"Dr. Irving said—"

"You never do anything you're not supposed to?"

Grace opened her mouth to tell her about the bell. But then Amy picked up a spoon and reached for the jelly jar again. "Delicious," she said, grinning at Grace.

"You're doing that on purpose," Grace said, "just because I told you not to." She turned her back and pulled off her jacket.

"You'd better stop acting so perfect," Amy said, "and help me do something about this kitchen instead."

Grace looked around. There were breakfast dishes on the table. Cereal was stuck to the bowls like paste and toast crumbs were sprinkled over the counter.

"Don't forget Fiona's coming," Amy said. She licked one of her fingers. "Fiona's coming on Sunday and when she walks in here, she's going to walk right out again." Amy laughed. "She's going to say the O'Malley kids live like goats." She shook her head. "Even Willie isn't as messy as we are."

Fiona. "I almost forgot," Grace said. She ran the water into the sink. How could she have forgotten? Fiona, her father's cousin, coming to visit all the way from Ireland.

At least her father *said* it was a visit. It probably wasn't a visit at all. She was probably coming to stay . . . to change everything around and tell them what to do.

Grace piled up the plates on the table and carried them over to the sink.

What *was* she going to do? Maybe she could glue the bell. Cement it together just the way her father had cemented the little gray-and-white dog for her mother that time it had fallen off the table.

Maybe she could tell her father. . . . She ran the sponge over one of the dishes. He was working late tonight and all day tomorrow. She rubbed at a yellow egg spot on the rim of the dish. And maybe he'd feel bad, sorry that she'd done something so awful, touched the bell, broke . . .

"Did you get your social studies book?"

Grace drew in her breath. "I forgot."

Amy raised her eyebrows and started to giggle. "Miss Perfect forgot something."

"It's not funny," she mumbled.

"But how . . . ?"

Grace shrugged. "Forget it." She went over to the table and started to wipe up the crumbs. She had gone back to school for nothing. She'd have to borrow Bianca's social studies book anyway. If only she hadn't gone back. She wanted to sit down and put her head on the table. Instead she threw the sponge into the sink. "Come on, Amy, let's go watch television."

3

Something was wrong. What was it?

Grace pulled the covers up around her chin. School? No, it was Saturday.

She listened to her father moving around downstairs and then the front door closed. He was on his way to work at Benton's, where he sold tools.

Her social studies book. She had forgotten it. She sat up straight. "That's nothing," she said. "I can go over to the bakery. Bianca will be helping her father today. I'll borrow . . ."

"What?" Amy mumbled from the bed next to her.

"Nothing." Then she saw her schoolbag hanging from its strap on the doorknob and remembered Mrs. Raphael's bell.

She swung her legs over the side of the bed and started to get dressed.

Downstairs in the kitchen a few minutes later, she took a container of orange juice out of the refrigerator and stood there looking at it. Someone had forgotten to close the top. There were little things floating around in the juice. She wondered if it was just ice, or pieces of orange, or . . .

At the window there was a scratching sound. She turned, knowing what she'd see.

A dirty brown dog, paws on the sill, was looking in at her.

"Are you here again?" she asked. She opened the door.

The dog padded in, banging his huge tail against the side of the cabinet.

She bent down and gave him a pat. "Listen, Buddy, I wish you'd find another place to live. Daddy said you can't stay here."

She cut up some leftover hamburger for him, then poured the orange juice into a glass and took it into the room behind the kitchen.

Her room.

Her father never had time to sit in there, and Amy said it was too cold, so she had fixed it up for herself.

She had shoved the old green chair with the chocolate-milk stain in front of the window and cut some horse pictures out of a magazine for the walls. Someday she was going to be a veterinarian, the kind that takes care of horses. She'd have animals all over the house and no one would complain if they shed a lot or had accidents. She looked up at the wall. Molly and Jo and Big Tom and Star had been thumbtacked there for so long that they were a little yellow-looking but still beautiful. She knew their faces as well as she knew her father's or Amy's.

She sat in the chair, looking out at Willie, while she finished her juice. She kept thinking about the bell. Somehow she had to fix it and get it back on Mrs. Raphael's desk before Monday morning.

Maybe she should tell Amy after all. Get her out of bed. She might be able to help.

Grace went into the hall to call her. She had to step over Buddy, who was crunched up in a ball at the foot of the stairs.

"You didn't," Grace said, wrinkling her nose.

Buddy stuck his nose under his paws and sighed.

"You did."

She looked into the living room. There was a dark wet patch in the corner of the rug.

"Hey, Amy," she yelled. "Buddy's wet the rug again. Come help me cover it up."

Amy clumped downstairs. "Any day now, we'll have to wear our boots when we want to sit in the living room."

"Very funny."

"We'll be able to sail a boat . . ."

"Help me move the chair over it." She cocked her head to one side and looked at the room. "The chair will look great over there and the last spot is good and dry by now."

Amy grabbed the arm of the chair and started to push it with her. "Someday Daddy is going to figure out why you move the furniture around so much. He's going to find out that a dog who looks like Dracula has his own private bathroom in the middle of our living room." Amy slid into the chair and started to laugh. "All he needs is a tub and a . . ." She was laughing so hard she couldn't get the rest of the words out.

Grace stood there watching her. Ordinarily she would have laughed too. But all she could think about now was the bell. And she could see it was no use to tell Amy. Amy would probably laugh and make some silly joke.

Amy sat up. "You know what we could do?"

"What?" Grace picked up the gray-and-white china dog from the corner table to look at the thin line of glue running around one of its legs. Then she went into the kitchen with Amy following behind her. She opened the junk drawer and fished around until she found the glue. The tube was a twisted mess, squeezed into a flattish ribbon.

Amy stood in the kitchen door. "We could go up to the fire tower."

She'd have to go to the shopping center and get some more glue. What if she couldn't fix the bell? What if . . . ?

"Want to?"

Grace glanced out the window. Outside it was cold and gray. "It looks like snow," she said.

"So what? Come on, Gracie."

"I have to go to the hardware store."

"All right. I tell you what. I've got a dollar. We can go to the shopping center on the way back from the lake. Stop at McDonald's for some french fries, or maybe we can go to Friendly's. Get some hot chocolate with whipped cream."

"I thought you weren't supposed to eat that stuff."

Amy made a face. "I'll have something else."

Please eat right, Grace wanted to say. She shook her head. She was always worried about Amy. Worried that she wouldn't eat enough and she'd get all funny and weak like someone who's drunk. Or worried that she'd eat too much and make herself sick the way she was before they knew she had diabetes.

"All right. I'll go with you," she said, thinking she'd stop in Sullivan's on the way back and get the glue. "I just have to feed Willie first."

She started for the back door. Buddy was lying in front of it. She let him out, then stepped out onto the back porch. In the corner was a trash bag full of dried-up leaves.

Willie loved their crunchy taste.

She pulled out a bunch and brought them over to the pen.

The goat was standing by the fence, waiting.

"Hey, Willie, old girl," Grace said. She reached inside the fence and patted Willie's head, thinking about the day Mr. Hunt had brought her last year.

Grace had been ten then, and Amy almost eight. Their mother had been dead only a couple of weeks. She remembered how small Willie had been. Grace had spent the whole day holding her because the goat kept crying for her mother.

Grace remembered knowing just how she felt. She had wanted her mother as much as Willie did. She wondered if Willie could remember her mother. The other day she had asked her father whether animals thought about their mothers, but he had only looked sad and rubbed the top of her head with his large hand.

She hadn't wanted to tell him that she could hardly remember her mother either.

Sometimes for a second she could almost see her mother's face. Then it would slip right out of her mind and she wouldn't be able to get it back again.

The first time it happened she had rooted through the dresser drawers to see if she could find a picture of her mother. But even though there were piles of pictures, they were mostly of herself and Amy, and even a few of her father. She guessed it was because her mother was the one who had always taken most of the pictures. The only one of her mother was so blurry, it was hard to tell what she looked like.

Grace pushed the leaves through the chicken wire, gave Willie's bony head a last pat, and went back into the house for her jacket.

4

She and Amy jogged along the dirt path on the other side of Mr. Hunt's field until they reached the road to the lake.

They went by the Virgos' summer cottage first. It was all boarded up and empty-looking. Then they passed the new house. It wasn't really new but it was the last one built on the lake road, so everyone called it that. The people who owned it didn't bother to board up the windows because they came for a weekend once in a while during the winter.

Next was Lisa Kile's house. Grace took a quick look down the driveway, hoping she wasn't outside, but she was.

"Hey," Amy said, "there's that new kid, Lisa."

"Nobody likes her," Grace said. "Don't ask—"

"I'll probably like her," Amy said. She grinned at Grace.

"Amy . . ." Grace began, but it was too late.

"We're going up to the fire tower," Amy yelled. "Want to come?"

Lisa had a ball in her hand. She threw it up in the air, caught it, then trotted over to them. She hadn't bothered to comb her hair and her eyelashes were covered with a yellow crust.

"Hi," Grace said, trying not to sound too friendly. She glared at Amy.

Lisa wiped one of her eyes, rubbed her hands on the sides of her jeans, and took off ahead of them. "Race you," she shouted.

Amy sprinted after her.

A moment later they turned up the curving road leading to the tower and disappeared.

Grace followed them slowly, kicking at the soggy brown leaves that matted the path, and listened to them yelling back and forth to each other.

When she got to the tower, she stopped to look up. She had to stretch her neck back to see all of it at once. She thought about the ninety-four steps she'd have to take, winding around, out in the open, to get to the top. It was really scary.

She could hear Amy and Lisa above her. Their feet clattered on the iron steps. Grace climbed slowly, thinking that Amy always got to the top first. Amy wasn't afraid of the stairs, or the wind that whistled around the platform.

Grace grasped the railing tighter, feeling the wetness of her hands.

When she reached the wooden platform on the top, Amy and Lisa were leaning against the railing, looking down. She stood next to them. Off to the side she could see Mr. Hunt's field and her own house with a little puff of smoke coming out of the chimney.

Below her the trees looked gray and wintry, and the lake seemed bare without the summer sailboats.

A little farther away was Danville. The streets looked like neat little squares. On Front Street she could see Bianca's father's bakery, and Benton's, where her father worked.

She shivered, feeling the wind, and pulled her jacket up around her neck. Then she watched the Amtrak train as it crossed the viaduct over the highway at the edge of town and passed the shopping center.

Today there were a dozen cars parked in the lot at the shopping center. People were running back and forth with bundles. Everyone was getting ready for Christmas next week.

Grace moved to the other side of the tower to look at the mountains. Behind her there was a strange noise. It sounded as if someone was trying to say something but it was coming out all mixed up.

"Hey, Amy," she heard Lisa say. "Are you all right?"

Grace turned in time to see Amy slide down to the floor of the platform. She sat there, crumpled up against one of the railing posts, staring at the sky.

She didn't look like Amy.

Grace could feel her heart begin to pound. She was next to Amy in a second, gripping her shoulders. "Amy? Did you eat breakfast?"

For a minute Amy didn't answer. Then finally she looked at Grace. "To-oast." She had trouble getting the word out. It looked as if she couldn't make her mouth do what she wanted it to.

"Not enough," Grace said. She felt as if she were going to scream. She tried to hold Amy up with one hand and fish through her pockets with the other. "Where are your Life Savers?" she asked.

Lisa put her face in between them. Her hair smelled a little like smoke. "What's going on?"

"I need something sweet," Grace said. "Sugar. Candy. Anything." She pushed at Amy so that she was resting against her instead of the post.

"What's the matter with her?" Lisa asked. "Is it catchy?"

"No. It's because of . . ." She closed her mouth, suddenly remembering that Amy hated everyone to know she had diabetes: "Don't you dare say one word about diabetes to anyone," Amy had said, "or I'll never speak to you again. Never."

"But why?" Grace had asked.

Amy had grabbed her arm. "I don't want people to think I'm some kind of a freak. Taking needles every day. Not allowed to have candy unless I feel weak. It sounds crazy."

Now Grace tried to think of something to tell Lisa. "Amy's on a diet," she said finally. "I guess she hasn't eaten in a couple of weeks."

"Weeks?" Lisa echoed.

"Well, days. Yesterday. Today." She could feel her voice getting louder. She didn't know what to do. They'd never get Amy down all those steps.

Maybe she could get Lisa to go down and get something. She could go to her house. Bring . . .

She swallowed. She didn't want to be left up there alone with Amy. She was afraid. Afraid that something would happen to Amy and she wouldn't know how to help.

And now she was afraid of Amy. She didn't seem like Amy at all. She was strange and scary-looking. And Grace wanted to run away somewhere and hide.

5

Before Grace could decide what to do, Lisa touched her shoulder. "Hold her," she said. "I'll go for something."

"Make it something sweet," Grace said. "Candy."

Lisa nodded quickly. Then she was gone.

Grace listened to her footsteps going down the iron stairs. Tapping. Like a dancer.

"I'll be back," Lisa yelled. "Right away."

And then Grace was left alone with Amy. The wind shrieked across the top of the platform and pulled at their clothes.

She looked down at Amy.

Last year, at first, they hadn't paid any attention to Amy. Her mother had been dead just a little while. And her father, who used to laugh and hug them all the time, was quiet now, hardly talking.

No one noticed what was happening to Amy . . . Amy sleepy all the time, Amy getting up, going to the bathroom five and six times in the middle of the night. Amy thirsty. Every day she ate more and every day she got skinnier.

Until finally everyone noticed at once. Mrs. Eberle, Amy's teacher, the kids in school, her father, and Grace. And then Dr. Irving.

Amy had been in the hospital for four days. When she came home, she had a whole set of rules she had to follow. And something called insulin.

"Perfectly simple," she said. "I put the insulin in a needle because I don't have any in my body. Stick the needle right in my leg. And *whoosh* I've got insulin like everybody else."

At first Grace thought it was horrible for Amy to have to give herself a needle. But then she found out that it didn't bother Amy. What bothered Amy was the diet.

"No candy, no cake, no soda," Amy said, mimicking Dr. Irving. "He says I can't digest sugar right. The only time I can have something decent like a Hershey bar is when I start to feel weak."

"But why . . ." Grace began, trying to understand.

Amy waved her hand around. "Go look it up in the library," she said. "I'm sick of thinking about the whole thing. Besides, I told you. It's perfectly simple."

Except it wasn't really so simple. Grace had heard Dr. Irving warning her father. Amy had to have exactly the right food. A perfectly balanced diet, he said. Too much of the wrong food and she could go into a coma. Too little food and she'd go into shock. Both bad. Both scary.

Now Amy mumbled something.

"It's all right," Grace said. She couldn't hear Lisa's footsteps anymore. She must be down off the tower.

In her mind Grace ran with her. Down the tower road. Onto Lake Road. Past the trees to her house. Into the kitchen and back out again.

"Toast," Amy said. She closed her eyes. Her face was white and damp with perspiration.

Grace didn't answer her. She waited for the sound of Lisa's feet again. It seemed to take forever. A few flakes of snow fell. They melted on the wooden platform.

At last Grace heard Lisa coming up the stairs. Slowly. She'd be out of breath.

The top of Lisa's head popped through the opening and she boosted herself up. She knelt down and emptied her pockets. A Hershey bar. A pack of cherry Life Savers. A bag of peanuts.

"Not the peanuts," Grace said. "There's not enough sugar in them." She tore open the Life Savers and poked two into Amy's mouth.

Amy raised her hand to her mouth but Grace pushed it away. "Suck on them," she yelled.

Grace sat back for a moment, watching the red

candy on Amy's tongue. Then Amy closed her mouth and began to suck.

Grace tore the rest of them out of the wrapper and fed them to Amy one by one. She watched as Amy's eyes began to look like Amy again. Watched her pull herself up so she was sitting straighter. "I'm all right," she said.

And finally she was. Slowly they went down the stairs and out on the road. Grace wanted to say, I hate you when you do this to me. But then she felt guilty. It wasn't Amy's fault that she had diabetes. "Why didn't you eat your breakfast?" she asked instead.

Amy frowned and glanced at Lisa. "Shut up, will you, Grace? It was just a little headache. Let's go down to the highway."

A few minutes later in Friendly's, Grace sipped at her hot chocolate. The whipped cream felt cool on her lips, but the chocolate was so hot it burned her tongue and made her eyes tear. She waited a little, then drank it. Amy and Lisa were telling sick jokes. They were laughing so hard that Amy kept spilling her diet soda.

Grace stood up. "I'm going next door to Sullivan's."

Amy looked up. "What for?"

She hesitated. "I have to get some stuff. Maybe I'll look around for some Christmas presents. I can't figure out what to get for Mrs. Raphael."

Lisa shook her head. "I'm not giving her anything."

Grace didn't answer her. Slowly she zipped up her

jacket, waiting to see if Amy was going to come with her.

"Besides," Lisa said in a loud voice, "she said we didn't have to give her a present."

Grace thought of the tree in the corner of the classroom with its little red bows and gold ornaments. "Children," Mrs. Raphael had said when she put it there, "if you can't afford to buy me a present, I'll be just as happy with a card. Make it yourself."

Grace made a face. She'd hate to be one of the ones who couldn't buy Mrs. Raphael a present. She'd hate to give her a stinky little card. Especially after what had happened yesterday.

"Are you coming, Amy?" she asked.

Amy took another sip of her soda. "In a minute. We'll catch up."

Grace walked over to Sullivan's Department Store. The store was small but the counters were crowded with things to buy. Mr. Sullivan always said he tried to keep as much as he could in stock so people wouldn't have to go all the way to the big mall in Binghamton.

Everything in the store was ready for Christmas. There were wreaths all over the place. Even the cash registers had plastic holly leaves pasted on them. "Jingle Bells" was blasting out of a loudspeaker somewhere.

Grace picked up a box of dusting powder and then a bottle of perfume. She looked at the perfume for a moment, then put it down again. She couldn't seem to think about Christmas shopping. All she could think of was the bell and the sound it made when it broke on the floor yesterday.

Finally she gave up.

She went to the hardware department in the back and bought a tube of cement glue, then went back outside to look for Amy.

6

After lunch Grace watched Amy cross Mr. Hunt's field on her way to her friend Janet's house.

Amy looked fine again, just the way she always did.

Grace ran upstairs for her schoolbag.

Downstairs again in the room in back of the kitchen she took the looseleaf package out of the schoolbag and spread it carefully on the floor. Then she sat down and stared at the broken pieces of the bell.

It looked as if she'd never get them back together again.

She could see one wing and the head but the rest of the pieces all looked alike. She picked them up one at a time and tried to fit them together.

Finally she found two that matched.

She reached for the glue and spread it along the edge

of one of the pieces. Then she put the two together and held them. The glue had a terrible smell. It made her eyes water.

After a minute she looked around for another piece to put with the first two. The one that fit was slightly rounded. She could see that she was working on the bottom of the bell. By the time she got to the fourth piece, her fingers were coated with half-dried glue. As she picked the piece up, it stuck to her fingers.

It took a long time before she was finally finished.

At last she sat back on her ankles and blew on the bell to make it dry faster. The glue looked thick and lumpy. The whole thing was terrible. All the cracks showed and there was a piece almost the size of her pinky nail that was missing from the bottom.

In the kitchen the back door slammed. "Amy?" she called.

"Janet's not home," Amy answered.

Grace slid the bell under the green chair, got up, and went out to the kitchen.

Amy threw her jacket on the counter and looked around. "Maybe we'd better do something about this house. It looks like Willie's pen."

Grace looked around. "It's not so bad. Just the lunch stuff."

"Wait till Fiona gets here tomorrow night. She'll think we wash the kitchen floor with a muddy mop."

"Too bad," Grace said.

"Hey, Gracie. What's the matter with you?"

Grace started to fill the sink with water. "Everything is always going wrong around here."

"Just because Fiona's coming?"

"Fiona Tierney. Whoever heard of a name like that anyway?"

Amy pulled the broom out of the closet. "It's not so bad."

"I'm probably going to hate her," Grace said. "And I hope she hates it here too. I hope she hates it so much, she turns around and flies right back to County Galway."

Amy leaned over to turn on the radio. She switched the dials around until she found some Christmas music. "I think it will be nice to have her here for Christmas."

Grace banged a plate into the dish rack. "I don't."

Amy looked at her, frowning. "I don't know why you're making such a big fuss. Daddy said it's only a visit. A couple of months. Just to straighten out this mess of a house."

"Daddy said he *thought* it would be a couple of months. That could mean years. Maybe even forever. I know what Daddy's thinking. He's probably thinking that in a year everything's gotten into a mess and we can't manage by ourselves."

Amy laughed. "He's right."

"He is not." Grace could feel the anger in her chest. "We're managing just fine. So what if the house is a little dirty?"

"Well, I think it's going to be excellent," Amy said. She started to sweep under the kitchen table. "Fiona will probably do all the dishes. And clean up too. We won't have to do anything around here anymore."

"You think everything is excellent all the time." Grace reached for the cereal box and poured a bunch of Froot Loops on the counter. She picked out the orange ones and ate them one at a time. "She's probably going to boss us around. Change everything." Suddenly she stopped chewing. "She'll probably want to sit at . . ." Grace began and broke off. Yes. Fiona would stand at the sink the way her mother had, and sit at her mother's place, and soon Grace wouldn't be able to remember her mother doing those things. It would be Fiona, a stranger, telling them what to do, and her mother would really be gone forever.

Grace went over to the table. "This would look better if we shoved it against the wall."

"Shove it against the wall and you won't be able to fit four people at the table."

"Yes, you will. Two people can sit on one side. Like you and me. Fiona can sit where you usually sit. Daddy can sit in his own place."

She leaned against the table and pushed it hard against the wall. Then she stood back. "Better."

Amy didn't say anything.

Grace looked at her out of the corner of her eye, but Amy was looking out the window, probably watching Willie eat.

"Hey," Grace said suddenly.

"What?"

"My room."

"That dinky little thing in back?"

"That's mine."

"So?"

"She has to sleep somewhere."

Amy's mouth opened with a little *oh*. "I bet Daddy didn't even think about where Fiona was going to sleep. It looks like a rat's nest in there and she's coming tomorrow night."

"I didn't mean that," Grace said. "I like the way it looks in there." She took another handful of cereal. She wondered why she hadn't asked her father to write to Fiona and tell her to stay right there in Galway. She should have begged him.

Grace looked at the little pot of ivy on the window ledge over the sink. There were only one or two leaves left and the rest of it was brown and dead-looking. Fiona would probably want to throw it out. And she'd throw out the cracked purple vase standing next to it too.

Grace could feel her eyes beginning to tear. Fiona wouldn't care that Grace had given the vase to her mother for her birthday last year or that her mother had loved the ivy.

She leaned over the sink and touched one of the leaves. "Oh, Amy," she said, "I don't want everything to be different."

But Amy wasn't there. She had grabbed up her jacket and gone out the back door. Grace could see her talking with her friend, Janet, at the edge of Mr. Hunt's field.

Grace poured a little water into the ivy, wondering what Fiona would be like. She tried to remember what her father had told them about her. He had looked up at the ceiling when Amy had asked the other night. "Terrific cook," he had said. "Scones . . . soda bread . . . prawns . . ."

"What's prawns?" Amy had asked, making a face.

"Shrimp. They're caught in the Corrib River. Right near where we lived. Best in the world." He was quiet for a minute.

"But what does she look like?"

He rubbed at the small bald spot in back of his head.

"Kind of skinny," he said. "Her one eye is a little . . ." He pointed to his own eye and shook his head. "I don't know. I haven't seen her in twenty-one years."

She was probably horrible.

Grace swept the cereal crumbs off the counter into the sink, then she went back into the little room behind the kitchen.

Skinny old Fiona would probably hate the green chair. And the horse pictures too. She'd want something neat and new.

Grace started to take the pictures down, digging at the thumbtacks with her fingernails. "It's not my fault," she said, "that you'll have to live in my closet now. Don't blame me. Blame Fiona Tierney."

She grabbed the chair. It was heavy. Really heavy. She pushed it a little way from the window and dragged it until she got it to the door.

That was as far as it would go. She gave it another shove, then she couldn't get it to move either way.

Finally she climbed over it and went back into the kitchen. She sucked on her middle finger. The edge of a thumbtack had gone under the nail.

The radio was still on. It sounded like a bunch of kids were singing Christmas carols. Through the window she could see it had started to snow. There was a little bit of white sticking to the grass.

She looked over toward Willie's pen. It was divided into two parts. In front was her porch, a fenced-in piece that she used for standing in the sun and looking around at the world. In back was her house. It was about half the size of the garage. It was full of soft warm hay.

Grace stood up on tiptoes. She couldn't see Willie, but Willie's gate was swinging back and forth. Willie was out of her pen again, probably heading toward Mr.

Hunt's field. Grace grabbed a bowl from the closet, filled it with cereal, and ran outside.

The wind whipped her hair against her face as she crossed the yard.

"Willie," she yelled. "Get back in here."

The goat looked over her shoulder but she kept going. She went over to see Mr. Hunt's goats every time she got loose.

Grace rattled the pan but Willie didn't pay any attention.

"Willie," she shouted, "I'm not kidding." She started to run.

By the time she caught up with her, Willie was starting across Mr. Hunt's field. Grace grabbed her by the collar. "Hey, don't you want something to eat?"

Slowly she turned Willie around and led her back to the pen.

She followed Willie inside and set the bowl down next to her. Then she snuggled into the hay to watch as Willie nosed into the cereal.

She could feel a lump in her throat. Everything was going wrong. She shivered and curled up a little closer to Willie.

The goat turned her head and looked at her with her pale green watery eyes. She edged a little closer to Grace and began to chew again. Grace could feel the warmth of her. The hay began to settle around Grace's shape and that became warmer too.

She closed her eyes. After a few minutes, a skinny Fiona appeared out of a dark place. As she came closer, Grace saw that her hands were cupped around the broken pieces of Mrs. Raphael's bell.

Grace tried to see her face, but Fiona's head was bent. She was looking at an angel's wing. It kept growing until it looked like a giant shrimp.

She could hear Buddy snapping his teeth and barking. He was pretending to be brave. "Poor Buddy," Grace kept saying. "He's afraid of Fiona."

Finally Fiona looked up at her. She had one eye in the middle of her forehead.

Grace began to cry. "It's not fair," she said. "I'm afraid too."

Then Willie moved against her. She opened her eyes with a start. "Just a dream," she said, curling her hand around one of the goat's ripply horns. Her mouth felt wet and gummy. She sat up and leaned against the rough wall, trying to make herself stay awake. She didn't want to go back to sleep and finish the dream.

7

On Sunday, Grace helped her father push the old chair across the yard and into the garage. Then she followed him back to the little room behind the kitchen.

"How did this place get into such a mess?" he asked, half to himself. "Look at these walls." He ran his hands over the thumbtack holes, then glanced at his watch. "We'll have to paint. Right away."

"I guess so," Grace said, thinking of the horses up in her closet.

"Spackle. And I think I've got a can of green downstairs. That means only one coat. We might just be able to do it before I have to leave for the airport. It dries fast." He looked at his watch again. "We've got about five hours. Want to help?"

"Yes. Sure."

"All right. Now get me some newspapers. And ask Amy to give us a hand. I'll go downstairs for the paint."

She went into the kitchen. Buddy was standing up on his back legs looking through the storm door. She opened the door a little and patted his dark brown head. "You'd better go away," she said. "Daddy still doesn't know you live here."

Then she went to the stairs. "Amy? Come on down. We're going to paint." She picked up a pile of newspapers from the hall table and went into the back room.

Her father had already begun. He was dabbing spackle into the thumbtack holes. He turned to look at her. "What would I do without you, Gracie?" he said.

She ducked her head, feeling embarrassed. She spread some newspapers over the bed in the corner. The sun shining through the window made bright patches on the wall and warmed her back. She looked up at her father and smiled. Then she put the last of the newspapers on the floor and went back to the stairs again.

"Amy," she yelled. "Come on."

She listened. "Amy?" Why didn't she answer? She could feel her heart start to thump a little. She went up the stairs, running the last few steps.

Amy was still in bed. She yawned when she saw Grace in the doorway.

"Didn't you hear me?" Grace leaned against the door. "I thought you were sick."

"Sick, smick," Amy said. "That's all you think about. I'm getting up right now."

Grace took a deep breath and waited for her heart to stop pounding. Then she went downstairs, through the kitchen, and into the back room to watch her father stir the paint.

It was the middle of the afternoon when they finished. "Step back and take a look," her father said.

"Spectacular," Amy said, her face full of paint.

Grace stood in the middle of the doorway, careful to stay away from the edges that were still damp.

It didn't seem like her room anymore. But even so it was beautiful. The flowers on the old bedspread looked bright against the light green paint. She frowned at the bare walls. Big Tom would have looked wonderful on the wall next to the closet, and Star over the bed.

She looked up at her father. "We did a great job," he said. He was smiling. "And we finished just in time."

She smiled back at him. "We'll clean up the brushes and stuff while you go to the airport."

Maybe everything would work out all right after all, she thought. She looked out at the sunny yard.

Buddy was walking around the garage. He stopped to sniff at something. Maybe Fiona would love dogs. Maybe she'd be thrilled to have a nice dog like Buddy in the house. They could teach him not to . . .

"We could really use a dog around here," she told her father a few minutes later, as he was leaving for the airport. "A watchdog, you know?"

Her father snorted. "That's all I need. Something else to worry about." He rubbed the top of his head. "And I don't think Fiona likes dogs." He opened the front door. "I'll be back in a couple of hours," he said. "As soon as I can."

Fiona. Who cared whether Fiona liked dogs? Grace stamped back into the green room.

Amy was curled up on the bed, looking at some comics in one of the old newspapers.

"Come on, Amy," she said irritably. "Let's get rid of this paint stuff."

"In a minute," Amy said, turning the page.

Grace picked up the brushes and went into the kitchen. At the sink she turned on the water. She watched it run over the brushes, turning the bottom of the sink into a green river and spattering the sides with pale greenish dots.

She stood there a long time, thinking about Fiona as the water became clearer and finally all the paint was gone. Behind her, Amy came in, crumpling the newspaper into large balls. "School tomorrow, blaah," Amy said. She stuffed the paper into a large bag.

Grace felt her heart turn over. The end of the weekend. She wished tomorrow would never come.

And then she remembered the punish work.

"Listen, Amy," she said, "I have to go to the bakery."

Amy nodded. "Get me a turnover or something."

Grace shook her head. "I've got to borrow Bianca's social studies book." She turned off the water. "I hope she's finished with it."

"Better hurry," Amy said. She looked at the clock over the sink. "They close at five."

"I know." Grace grabbed her jacket off the chair and opened the back door. "Put the brushes away, will you? I'll be back soon."

She went past Willie's pen, clicking her teeth at the goat, then started across Mr. Hunt's field. It would be dark soon. And it was getting cold. She jammed her hands into her pockets and began to run.

When she was almost there, she could see the lights of the bakery spilling out onto Front Street. It was the only store that was open. She hurried down the street and went inside.

Bianca was wiping crumbs off the counter. She looked up and smiled when she saw Grace. She reached under the counter for a chocolate chip cookie and handed it to her. "I helped my father make them," she said. "They're pretty good."

Grace bit into it. "Terrific. Thanks." She leaned against the counter. "Did you finish your social studies questions?"

Bianca made a face. "They were hard, but we weren't busy today so I finished them a little while ago."

"I forgot my book," Grace said, wondering what Bianca would think if she knew that she had gone back into the classroom and broken the teacher's bell. For a moment she thought about telling her. But suppose Bianca thought it was terrible? Suppose . . .

"Want my book?" Bianca asked.

"Do you mind?"

Bianca shook her head. "It's a good thing you caught me. My father's getting the bread set for the morning, then we're going to close a few minutes early. You would have been out of luck."

While Bianca went into the back to get the book, Grace looked at the trays. She tried to decide which she liked best. There really wasn't much left. An apple cake, some cookies, and a tray of bagels. Bianca was really lucky. She probably had cake for dessert every night.

She thought about Fiona. Daddy had said she'd have her dinner on the plane and that he'd grab something at the airport. She and Amy were having TV dinners again. But maybe she should bring some cake home. She could set the table in the dining room.

Bianca handed her the book. "I hope you get it all finished." She leaned over closer. "How's Amy?"

"Amy? Fine."

"Lisa came in for some bread yesterday and she said . . ."

"You mean about on the tower?"

Bianca nodded. "Lisa said she fainted. She said she probably wasn't getting enough to eat. That maybe you were poor."

Grace felt her face redden. "I didn't tell her that Amy had diabetes. She wasn't here when Amy was in the hospital and Amy hates everyone to know."

"I told her," Bianca said. She handed Grace another cookie and took one for herself. "My father said my aunt has diabetes too. He said a lot of people have it." She hesitated. "I don't understand it, though. Amy's never allowed to have candy. But Lisa said that up on the tower—"

"I gave her candy," Grace finished for her. She took a deep breath. "I had to look it up in the library. Miss Bailey, the librarian, helped me."

She leaned against the counter. "If a person without diabetes eats something, say, a piece of bread, then he'll have exactly the right insulin so he can digest it. Right?"

"I guess so."

"Well, if a kid has diabetes, he gets a set amount of insulin in a needle. Then he's supposed to have an exact amount of food so he won't have too much or too little insulin running around inside him. If he eats too little, he gets sick because he has all that extra insulin. If he eats too much, he gets sick because he doesn't have enough insulin."

"But—" Bianca began.

"Amy got sick up there on the tower because she had too much insulin. She didn't bother to have any breakfast. So she had to have candy quick. To get rid of all that extra insulin. See?"

Bianca closed her eyes and thought. "I guess so," she said again.

"Well, that's it. And we're not poor. That Lisa had some nerve."

Bianca wiped the crumbs off her mouth. "I told her you weren't poor. Lisa's not poor either," Bianca said.

"That's what I thought. My father said . . ." She raised her shoulders. "They're just different. He said her mother and father don't care about being clean or wearing nice clothes. They don't care much about anything. Neither does Lisa, I guess."

Absently, Grace pointed to the apple cake. "Will you wrap that up for me?" she asked. "Put it on my father's bill." She tucked the book under her arm. "I'll give this back to you tomorrow."

Poor, she thought again as she opened the bakery

door. That crazy Lisa. How terrible it would be not to care about anything.

It was really dark outside. She held the cake box carefully with one hand, and put the other in her pocket. Then she started to run toward home.

8

As soon as they finished their TV dinners, Grace dug around in the closet until she found her mother's best white tablecloth.

She ran her hands over it, thinking of her mother ironing it every year at Christmas. Her mother would drag out the ironing board, grumbling about how she hated to iron, complaining that the tablecloth wasn't worth all that work. But halfway through she'd be singing Christmas carols.

Grace could almost hear the sound of her mother's voice. She closed her eyes tight, concentrating as hard as she could, trying to see what her mother's mouth looked like, trying to remember.

Amy leaned over her shoulder. "That's a wrinkled mess."

Grace opened her eyes. "We can smooth it out with

our hands. When we get some plates on the table and put the cake in the middle, it won't look bad at all."

She picked up the tablecloth and went into the dining room.

"How about candles?" Amy asked. "There are some yellow ones in the kitchen drawer."

Grace nodded. "Terrific. That Fiona will see we know what we're doing. That we don't need her around here one bit."

From the kitchen Amy called back. "No, we don't need Fiona. I can just keep on eating little burnt TV peas until I'm grown up."

Grace grinned at her as she appeared in the doorway. "We had that only once this week."

"Hamburgers four other days."

Grace took a pile of books off the table and spread the cloth on it. "Now we'll be eating those prawn shrimps four times a week." She went to the china closet and took out the plates.

"Beautiful," Amy said a moment later as she put a candle on each end.

Grace tugged at the end of the cloth to straighten it a little, then, satisfied, she went back into the kitchen for Bianca's social studies book and a piece of looseleaf.

It took her a long time to do all the questions, but still Fiona and her father hadn't come. She and Amy waited in the big chair next to the living-room window, yawning.

Finally the car lights swept across the front of the house, and they heard the noise of the car coming up the driveway. They looked at each other. "I hope she's pretty," Amy said.

Grace shook her head. "I hope Daddy's alone. Maybe she didn't come."

Then the car door opened. Grace turned to look. From the light inside the car she could see that Fiona Tierney wasn't pretty. She wasn't skinny either. She was fat, especially around the middle, and old-looking. Her hair was mostly gray and frizzy and looked as if it hadn't been combed in a week. She came around the car, walking kind of sideways, trying to hold on to a bunch of brown paper packages.

Grace went to open the door. As Fiona started up the steps, she could see what her father meant about her eye. It turned out just a little bit. When she smiled, Grace couldn't be sure if she was looking at them or at something off to one side.

Fiona stopped in the hallway and put her hand under Grace's chin. "You're Grania," she said.

"No—Grace."

"It's all the same in the Irish," Fiona said. "Grace is Grania." She reached into one of the paper bags and handed a necklace to Grace and another one to Amy. "Made of turf," Fiona said. "I don't know what they'll think of next, I don't."

"What . . ." Grace began as Amy slipped hers over her head.

"The very earth," she said, "baked and molded and written on. And a string to tie around your neck. I hope you like them."

By this time her father had picked up Fiona's suitcase and was leading them toward the green room. He stopped at the dining-room door. "What's this?"

"We've got cake for you," Amy said. "For Fiona, I mean. Grace took out the best tablecloth and—"

"Here," their father said. He took the rest of the packages out of Fiona's arms and put them on the hall table. "That's nice, girls. I'll bet Fiona would love a cup of tea."

Amy reached out for Fiona's hand. "See? Candles and everything." Then she looked back at Grace. "It was Grace's idea. She bought the cake."

Grace put the turf necklace down on the hall table and followed them into the dining room. "It wasn't anything," she said. She wished Amy wasn't making such a fuss. Let Fiona think they always ate this way. She frowned a little at Amy to make her keep quiet, but Amy didn't seem to notice. She was still telling Fiona about the cake.

Grace closed her eyes. Cake. She had forgotten to get something Amy could eat. If only she had gotten a bagel for her.

She saw Amy grinning at her. "I guess I'll have to take a little piece of cake," Amy said. "There's nothing else." She held out her fingers and measured. "Just the tiniest . . ."

"Amy . . ." her father began.

"I never saw a table set so pretty," Fiona said. "For me, is it? And maybe we could have a wee piece of toast with a little apple on it? I make it that way at home. Maybe Amy would like to try it."

"It sounds good," Amy said.

Grace stared at Fiona. Fiona must know about Amy's diabetes. And she had thought about the apples right away. Already Amy was running out to the kitchen to get some.

Grace swallowed hard. "Sit down," she said stiffly. "I'll get some tea." She started toward the kitchen. "I don't want any help," she told Fiona over her shoulder.

A few minutes later she was back, holding the teapot as carefully as she could, determined not to spill one drop. She sat down slowly and reached for Fiona's cup.

"Well now," Fiona said. "You've got the map of Ireland right on your face." She leaned over and pushed back Grace's bangs.

"Map?"

Her father grinned. "It means you look Irish."

"And something else. You're just the way I picture her."

"My mother?"

"Glory no." She looked at Amy and smiled. "Amy's like Katie, your mother. You're like the other Grace O'Malley. The Pirate Queen. She was a fierce one all right. Brave and bold."

"Grace?" Amy said, her voice sliding up. "Brave and bold?" She started to giggle.

Grace began to cut the cake. "I never heard of her."

Fiona turned to Grace's father. "These girls don't know about Grace O'Malley?"

He shook his head. "I guess not."

"Or the *White Sea Horse?*"

"I don't think . . ."

"Brian Boru, the chief of the O'Kenedy clan?"

He grinned. "No."

"Shame on you, Fenton," she said. "It's a good thing I'm here." She turned back to Grace and Amy. "I hope you've heard of St. Patrick at least."

Grace nodded, looking at Amy. Amy's face was red from trying not to laugh.

"Well, that's something anyway," Fiona said. She stared up at Grace's father. "And do you remember," she said, "the time we went all the way down to Longford to see Katie's cousin jump?"

Grace looked first at Fiona, then back at her father. It seemed strange to hear anyone talking about her mother. Katie. She never even thought of her mother having a name like everyone else.

"We skipped school," her father said.

"And Katie was afraid to go with us. She was afraid she'd get caught," Fiona said.

"The cousin's horse won the jump," her father said. Fiona nodded.

"And even though we got in trouble, Katie was mad she hadn't come."

Suddenly Grace thought she saw tears in her father's eyes. He pushed his chair back and stood up. "I have to get something from the kitchen," he said. "Milk . . ." His voice trailed off.

Grace could see the pitcher of milk in the center of the table. She looked down at her plate.

Fiona stood up. She held her arms out to him, and for a moment they rocked back and forth together.

"I'm that sorry about Katie," Fiona said. "I always loved her."

He shook his head and patted Fiona's arm. Then he went out to the kitchen.

Fiona loved her mother? Grace looked at her as she pulled the chair back and sat down heavily.

"My mother's ivy is in the kitchen," Grace said, not sure why she wanted to tell Fiona that. "It looks horrible, almost dead."

At first Fiona didn't answer. Then she said softly, "Well, suppose we take a look at it tomorrow or so? Maybe it needs something. More earth or . . ."

Then her father was back.

Fiona looked up at him. "You look as good as gold, me boy," she said. "You'd hardly see the little bald spot in back of your head."

Grace bit her lip, trying not to smile. Her father hated to hear anything about being bald.

But her father didn't seem to mind. He smiled and shook his head up and down as Fiona began to talk a mile a minute.

"Cousin Bridey McGowan down the road was fit to be addled that I was coming out to America instead of her. 'Now, now,' I said to Bridey, 'you've had your share of children and I've spent half a lifetime taking care of the rectory for Father Reardon, the priest. Cooking the meals and cleaning the house . . .' when I should have been married years ago, I guess. Married to . . ." She shook her head and laughed. "A couple of people asked me. But the only one I liked was Tom. . . . I can't even remember his last name now. He wasn't such a great bargain though." She smiled at them. "Now I'll take care of my own."

Grace drew in her breath. "How long are you staying?" she asked, not looking at Fiona or her father.

"A month or so," said her father.

Then Fiona put her hand on Grace's shoulder. "Just for a bit. Just to help you out a little. And to let Janie Curry find out that working for Father Reardon isn't as easy as it looks."

Grace felt herself smiling. "Fiona," she said. "There's something I'd like to ask you."

"And why not?"

"What do you think about animals?"

"Animals? Tigers and such?"

"No. I mean . . ."

"She means dogs," Amy said. "Ugly-looking dogs."

"Not ugly," Grace said.

Fiona shook her head. "Don't get me near those devils. Ugly or not. I've had enough of dogs to last me a lifetime."

9

On Monday morning Grace woke up early. She lay there thinking about last night and Fiona. She should have known Fiona wouldn't like dogs. She probably wouldn't like goats either. Maybe she'd hate it here and end up going home. Good.

Then she thought about school and suddenly remembered the bell. She could feel a lump in her chest. What was she going to do? She slid her legs out of the side of the bed and stood up.

A few minutes later she tiptoed past her father's door, still buttoning her sweater. She could hear her father snoring gently.

Downstairs she hesitated in the hall. She could hear the noise of pots banging together and the sound of water running. Fiona must be up.

Grace didn't want to see her. She unlocked the front

door as quietly as she could and went outside. Buddy's footprints were all over the place: muddy little circles on the snowy path and up on the porch. She clicked her teeth and whistled for him, but he was nowhere in sight.

She ducked around the side of the house and let herself into Willie's pen. "Sorry," she said, giving her a pat on the shoulder. "I didn't bring your breakfast yet."

She ran her hand over Willie's coarse white hair, thinking about school and what was going to happen. Mrs. Raphael would be standing at the door the way she always did, watching everyone come in. But today she'd be wondering who broke the bell.

Grace could picture Mrs. Raphael's eyes on her, staring, making Grace open her mouth and tell the truth.

She drew in her breath. She wouldn't look at Mrs. Raphael. She'd keep her eyes on the floor or on Carol Betz, who sat in front of her. Or maybe she'd make believe she didn't feel well, that she had a fever. Then Mrs. Raphael would think she looked strange because of the flu and not because she was the one who had broken the bell.

She gave Willie one more pat. "I'll bring your breakfast in a few minutes," she said. "I have to get ready for school."

Slowly she walked back across the yard and opened

the door to the kitchen. Everything sparkled. The counters were clean and there were no drips on the stove. Even the floor was clean and shining. The kitchen looked the way it used to when her mother was there. She bit at her lips. Already Fiona was taking over.

Fiona was standing at the stove. She turned when Grace came into the kitchen. A dish towel was wrapped around her hand so she could hold a steaming frying pan. A soda bread was sticking out of the top of the pan. It looked like a fat brown sun with raisin eyes.

Fiona beamed at her.

Grace tried to think of something to say. "Didn't you go to bed last night?" she asked finally.

"Of course I did, macushla. But I didn't sleep for too long. At home the time is different. Right now it would be lunchtime, at least."

Grace went over the cabinet and scooped some of Willie's feed into a bowl. "I wish it was lunchtime here," she muttered. "Or tomorrow. Or next summer."

"Are you wishing your life away?" Fiona asked as she turned the bread out of the pan.

Grace shrugged. "I have to feed Willie."

"Willie?"

"My goat. I'll leave her bowl at the back door so I won't forget to take it out for her after breakfast."

She sat down, waiting for Fiona to say something about Willie and how she hated animals. But Fiona just smiled and sat down across from her. She began to cut thick wedges of bread. "Isn't it nice," she said, "to be here together. To get to know each other."

Grace didn't answer. She picked up a piece of bread and reached for the butter. She felt mean inside and uncomfortable. She tried not to look at Fiona, but finally she glanced up. Fiona was still smiling at her, waiting for her to take the first bite of soda bread.

"I knew it," Fiona said. "And now that I see you clearly I'm sure. You're just like a picture of Grace O'Malley I saw once." She cocked her head to one side. "Well, not really a picture. It was carved out of wood."

"Really?"

Fiona nodded. "Your mother never told you about her?"

Grace frowned, trying to remember. Then she shook her head.

"Well now," Fiona said. "Someday I'll tell you a story about her."

"A pirate queen?" Grace said. She took another bite of her bread, thinking she didn't care about pirate queens or wood carvings or old stories or . . .

"A pirate queen?" Amy echoed from the doorway. "Tell us now."

Fiona stood up and poured a glass of juice for Amy. She looked back at Grace and hesitated for a moment. "You have to think of the sea. And the gray cold mist of the west of Ireland. The water is black and rough and the wind moans across the rocks. It is a desolate place. Can you see it? Can you hear the wind?"

"I can see it," Amy said.

"Now see a woman. She is tall and straight and beautiful. She stands in front of her castle, looking out at the sea. She loves the cold and the mist and the feel of her red velvet dress swirling about her. She owns the rocks on which she stands and the sea in front of her and no ship will dare to enter her territory. She is Grania O'Malley, the Pirate Queen."

Fiona reached out and touched Grace's cheek with one finger. "And you, Grace O'Malley, you too are Grania. You and the Pirate Queen come from the same heritage, from the same fierce Irish chieftains."

Grace took a deep breath and blinked.

Fiona sat back and nodded.

"Her castle is standing there still, on Clew Bay," Fiona said. "I saw it with my own eyes. The windows were great high slits in the rock. And do you know what?"

Grace swallowed. "What?"

"She had a rope," Fiona went on. "One end was attached to her favorite ship, the *White Sea Horse,* and the other end went right up the castle wall through her bedroom window. Some people say it was attached to her bedpost. Others say it was attached to her ankle.

Her sailors would pull on the rope if a pirate ship was sighted. It would wake her and she'd—"

Suddenly Fiona stood up, knocking the chair over backward. "Saints preserve us," she yelled. "It's the devil himself looking in the window."

Grace looked up and gulped. Buddy was standing there, looking in, his front two paws on the sill.

"It's just my dog," she said. She could hear Amy sputtering with laughter.

"Dog? Fenton didn't tell me you had a . . ."

"Well, he's not exactly ours."

Fiona was glaring at Buddy. "I'm glad he's not yours. Shoo," she yelled at the dog through the window. "He's a mean-looking one, he is."

Grace looked at Amy. Amy's face was red from trying to hold in her laughter and her eyes were dancing. "I have to go to the bathroom," she said, and dashed out of the kitchen.

"Buddy? Mean?" Grace said as she watched the dog bound off the porch and into the yard. She turned back to Fiona. "He'd probably take your arm right off."

She slid out of her chair. Somehow Fiona's frightened look made her feel worse instead of better. "I have to feed Willie," she muttered.

"You'd better not go out there now," Fiona said. "Suppose that monster dog is out there?"

"Don't worry," Grace said. "I'm not afraid." She grabbed up Willie's bowl and went out the back door.

Twenty minutes later Grace crossed the yard ahead of Amy, carrying her notebook in one hand and fresh water for Willie in the other.

"Wasn't that nice," Amy said, "that Fiona kissed us good-bye this morning?"

Grace raised one shoulder.

"You know, Grace?"

Grace slowed down. "What?"

"I like that Fiona. I like the way she cooks and the way she talks. I even like the look of her."

Grace glanced at her quickly. "Mother was a much better cook."

Amy shrugged. "Don't worry. As soon as we get used to Fiona, she'll probably go back to Ireland. She'll forget all about us."

"Good."

"Do you know what she said?"

Grace set the bowl down inside the pen. "What?"

Amy put one hand on her hip. "That girl," she said, trying to sound like Fiona, "is brave and bold. I don't think she's afraid of anything. She went right out there with that devil of a dog waiting to sink his mouth into someone's ankle."

"She said that?" Grace asked, a warm feeling spreading through her chest. She tucked her notebook under her arm.

"And wasn't that a great story about that queen? What was her name?"

"Grania."

"Right. Same as yours, Fiona said. Wouldn't it be wonderful if we were related? Way back. Fiona says you look like her."

"Don't be silly. We're not related." For a moment Grace could see the queen in her red dress, standing by the sea, not afraid, never afraid, not worrying about pirates or . . .

"Hey. Ya-hoo," a voice said.

Grace looked up. Lisa Kile was headed toward them.

"That goat's a beauty," she said.

Grace frowned. Lisa's hair was hanging in her face. She probably hadn't bothered to comb it again. "What are you doing here?"

"Can I go in the pen?" She opened the chicken-wire fence. "I got up early." She waved her hand around. "I go all over the place." She bent down and put her arms around Willie's neck. "Lu-cky," she said, drawing the word out. "What's her name?"

"Her name is Wilhelmina," Grace said shortly.

"Come on, you guys," Amy said. "We'll be late for school."

Grace stood waiting as Lisa came out of the pen, then closed the gate as Lisa ran to catch up with Amy. From the corner of her eye she could see Fiona at the kitchen window. She turned to get a better look. Fiona was waving and smiling at them.

For a minute she wasn't going to wave back. Then she raised her hand for a moment and started to run after Lisa and Amy.

10

"Grace O'Malley. Brave and bold," Grace whispered to herself as she followed the rest of the class up the stairs to the sixth-grade room.

Mrs. Raphael was standing at the door as usual, waiting for them. She nodded to each one of them. "Good morning," she said every few seconds.

Grace ducked her head as she went by and didn't look up again until she had reached her own desk. Then she glanced up at Mrs. Raphael from under her eyelashes. But Mrs. Raphael didn't look any different from the way she usually did on Monday mornings.

Grace pulled a pencil out of her desk and began to pick at it to sharpen the point. She watched Andrew Smith across the aisle hitch his desk away from Lisa Kile's, but Lisa wasn't paying any attention to him. She had her head back, looking at the ceiling. Her lips were moving a little. Grace wondered if she was talking to herself or singing something under her breath.

"All right," Mrs. Raphael said. "We're going to do things a little differently today. We're going to start with a composition."

Grace sighed. She'd never minded doing compositions when she was in fifth grade, but this year she had to keep her sentences short and stick to easy words because Mrs. Raphael counted everything.

Mrs. Raphael pushed her hair back. "I want you to write a composition," she said, "about . . ." She paused and looked out the window. "Well, let's see, how about losing something you loved?"

Grace took out a piece of paper. She stared at the paper, trying to think of something to write about.

Next to her, Andrew began to talk to the boy in front of him. "I lost my pants once," he whispered.

Edward Gardner looked back and grinned. "Lisa Kile lost her soap."

"Lisa Kile never had any soap."

Grace thought of her horses, dusty and locked away in the top of her closet.

As neatly as she could, she wrote across the top of the paper: THE DAY I LOST MY HORSE.

Then she stopped and bit at her pencil point. How could you lose a horse? Maybe one could run away. Or die. Or maybe if you were poor, you'd have to sell one.

"You're dreaming, Grace O'Malley," Mrs. Raphael said. "Five minutes more, class."

It better be the poor idea. There was no time to think of anything else.

Grace stared at the paper for a minute, then she wrote:

> Once upon a time the Smith family was poor. There was no food. There was no money. There was no heat in the house. The father had to sell their horse. The children were crying. The horse was sad. But what could they do?

Mrs. Raphael looked at her watch. "Stop," she said in a loud voice. "I want to save a little time so that some of us can share our compositions with the rest of the class."

Andrew groaned.

"Mine isn't finished," someone in the front said.

Mrs. Raphael shook her head. "You had ample time." She looked around the room.

Grace bent her head over her paper. She usually ducked behind Carol Betz. But Carol was absent today so there was a big empty space in the row. Grace could almost feel Mrs. Raphael staring at her.

"Lisa Kile," said Mrs. Raphael.

Lisa picked up her paper and began to read. "I lost so many things I can't remember them all. But once

I lost a blue sweater. My mother was mad. She . . ." Lisa's voice trailed off.

Mrs. Raphael waited for a minute. "Is that all?" she asked.

Lisa nodded. "All I had time for."

"Disgraceful," Mrs. Raphael said. She looked around again. "Let's hear yours, Bianca."

Bianca stood up. Her face was a little red because Mrs. Raphael had called on her. But it made her look even prettier than usual.

Grace sat back while Bianca read her composition. It was really good. She had written about a little gold ring her grandmother had given her, and how she felt when she had lost it.

After Bianca sat down, Mrs. Raphael stood there smiling for a few seconds. "Yes," she said, "that's the kind of thing I'm looking for."

Grace looked down at her desk. It seemed as if Mrs. Raphael had called on Bianca just to show everyone how awful Lisa Kile's composition had been.

Mrs. Raphael moved a step closer to Grace's aisle, looking past the empty space right at Grace. "Grace O'Malley. Let's see what you have to say."

Grace cleared her throat and stood up. She hated to read anything out loud. Her voice always sounded too high and she stopped in all the wrong places.

"The day I lost my horse . . ." she began.

"Boo hoo," Edward said to Andrew.

Grace raised the paper closer to her face so she couldn't see anybody in the room, then she read the composition as fast as she could.

"She never had a horse," Andrew said as she sat down. "She should have written about the day she lost her mind."

Mrs. Raphael flicked at her hair with one finger. "What did you say, Andrew?"

Andrew's face reddened. "Nothing," he said after a second.

"I'm waiting," Mrs. Raphael said, frowning.

"I said that Grace O'Malley never had a horse."

"She has a goat," Lisa Kile said, twirling her hair around her finger. "A beautiful goat."

Grace stared down at a little triangle someone had dug into her desk with a pencil. She could hear one of the boys laughing in front of the room.

"*Maah*," Edward said under his breath.

"That will do," Mrs. Raphael said. She waited until the class was quiet. "Do you have a horse, Grace?"

Grace looked up and shook her head. She wanted to say that she wasn't lying about the horse. Her fifth-grade teacher, Miss Patterson, had said it was all right to make things up for compositions. It was like telling stories, Miss Patterson had told them, or writing books.

Mrs. Raphael blinked. "Then why did you . . ."

"I made it up. . . ." Grace began, and stopped.

Mrs. Raphael frowned. "Next time, write the truth.

That's the trouble, people just don't tell the truth." She clamped her mouth shut. "Pass the papers up to the front," she said.

Then Mrs. Raphael walked to her desk and picked up a paper. "I wrote a composition too," she said as she turned back toward them. "I want to read it to you."

Suddenly everyone in the class was still. No one fiddled with pencils, or papers, or moved their chairs around. Grace looked up at Mrs. Raphael. She felt her heart begin to pound. The bell, she thought.

"Many years ago," Mrs. Raphael said, looking down at her paper, "my first class gave me a bell. Whenever I looked at that bell, I thought about the children in Warwick. I remembered how happy I was when I was a new teacher. Every Christmas I put the bell on my desk so that all the children could enjoy looking at it."

Mrs. Raphael looked up at them. Grace could see that her eyes looked shiny. She wondered if Mrs. Raphael was crying.

"And then," Mrs. Raphael said, her voice uneven, "someone took the bell. Deliberately. Now no one will be able to enjoy the spirit of Christmas the bell brought to the sixth-grade classroom."

11

The day seemed to take forever to be finished. Grace didn't talk to anyone unless she was sure Mrs. Raphael was busy with someone else. And she didn't go near Mrs. Raphael, not even for help with her math.

Instead she kept her head down over her work, just looking up once in a while to stare out the window at the tiny grains of snow that swept sideways across the schoolyard.

At last the three o'clock bell rang. Quickly she gathered up her books and her jacket. She was first in line to leave the classroom.

Outside she scooped up a little mound of snow from the sidewalk and threw it at the flagpole.

"Wait up," Lisa Kile called behind her. "I'll walk you home."

Grace made believe she didn't hear her. She crossed over to the other side of the street.

"Hey, Gracie," Lisa yelled.

Grace hurried toward the corner. She could hear Lisa's footsteps pounding up behind her.

"What is it?" she asked, wondering if everyone in the class was standing out in front, watching her talk to Lisa Kile. She looked over her shoulder. There was a line waiting to get on the school bus. Bianca was standing there, talking to some of the kids. She spotted Grace and waved.

She turned back to Lisa uncomfortably. "I have to go now," she said.

"Want to go to McDonald's with me?" Lisa asked. She pulled at her hat. It was old and purplish and the wool had pilled up into little balls. "I've got some money for a Big Mac."

"Can't," Grace said, feeling angry at Amy. It was all her fault. Before the day at the tower Lisa had never bothered with her. Now it seemed that Lisa was determined to hang around her and let everyone think they were friends.

"I thought the day would never be over," Lisa said.

Grace closed her eyes for a second, feeling the snow against her lashes.

"I bet she thinks I took her old bell," Lisa went on. "I always get blamed for everything."

Grace didn't answer. She shifted her notebook to her other arm.

"You'd think that bell was worth about a hundred dollars."

"Well, I guess it was pretty expensive if her first class bought it for her. They probably chipped in."

"Eight fifty-eight," Lisa said.

"No. More. Lots more."

"I told you. Eight fifty-eight."

Grace swallowed. "How do you know?"

"I saw it in a store."

"You saw it?" Grace repeated. "Eight fifty-eight?"

Not such a terrible amount of money. She still had about four dollars left for Christmas presents. There'd be tax. Maybe Amy would lend her some, or her father.

"Where did you see it?" she asked as casually as she could.

"Who cares? I don't have that much money. Even if I did, I wouldn't buy it for her."

"But where—"

"Let's go over to the shopping center. To McDonald's," Lisa said. "Maybe I'd remember."

Grace pushed her hair behind her ears. She could feel Lisa's eyes on her. "Well, maybe for a few minutes. Just for something quick."

Lisa grinned. "Good. I'll treat. I have enough for sodas too."

"Where did you see the bell?" Grace asked again.

"Why do you want to know about that?" Lisa picked up a fistful of snow with one hand and threw it ahead of her into the street.

"I was just wondering."

Lisa didn't answer. By this time they had reached the viaduct where the train crossed the highway. It was colder walking under it. Grace could hear the dripping of the icicles as they melted down from the stone overhead.

Lisa shouted to hear her echo. "Try it," she told Grace. "Let's see what your voice sounds like."

Grace raised her voice and yelled once. Then she did it a few more times and they were out of the tunnel. "The bell?" she prodded Lisa.

"I forget," Lisa said.

"Are you sure it was the same? Did it have the angel on top?"

Lisa nodded impatiently.

"Pink? Was it pink?"

Lisa twitched her shoulders impatiently. She hitched her books up under one arm, then suddenly reached out, snatched Grace's notebook, and ran.

Grace stood there for a moment. She could feel a little point of anger in the middle of her chest. If it weren't for the bell, she'd turn around and go back home. She really didn't need the notebook until tomorrow. She could copy her science homework on a piece of looseleaf.

She kicked at a clump of snow that lay in the path ahead of her and followed Lisa slowly to the highway.

Lisa was standing at the counter in McDonald's when she got there. She swiped at Grace's shoulder and handed her the notebook. "Why didn't you run?"

Grace looked at her notebook. There was a smudgy fingerprint next to her name on the front cover.

"I ordered for you," Lisa said. "A Big Mac and some fries."

Grace rubbed at the print as the woman set their order down in front of them.

She followed Lisa to a booth. "What about the bell?"

"Well," Lisa said. She grabbed some french fries out of the white paper package. "My mother took me into Binghamton. To the big mall. There's a china store there. You know? I saw it on a shelf."

Grace took a sip of soda. Binghamton. It was thirty miles away. With all that extra overtime he worked, she'd never get her father to take her there before Christmas.

12

Grace had just finished her homework when she heard footsteps in the driveway.

"It's your father," Fiona said. "Poor man, it's almost nine o'clock. Run and take his coat, Amy," she said. "And, Grania, help me. I have a little surprise."

A moment later her father came in the back door, brushing snow off his shoulders. "It's cold out there," he said.

"Well," said Fiona, "it's time for something hot to warm you. Pears and apricots poached in their own juice. Nice and hot with a little stick of cinnamon."

He rubbed his hands together. "Sounds good."

"Mother used to make that," Grace began, and bit her lips.

"I thought we'd have it in the living room," Fiona said. "I've laid a fire. All it needs is the flame."

"Fiona, you're a wonder," he said as he followed her into the living room.

"Bring some spoons, Grania love, and napkins," Fiona called over her shoulder.

Grace brought in a pile of napkins and put them on the end table, then she handed the spoons to Fiona. She sat down with Amy on the floor in front of the fireplace and watched as her father took a long taper off the mantel and bent over to light the fire.

After a moment the fire flared up, casting long shadows against the wall. The room glowed in the orange light.

"Beautiful," Fiona said. "And I love the way the furniture is. Different, you know. Not all piled up against the wall." She waved her arms around. "The blue chair in the middle of the rug and the couch . . ."

"The girls did that," her father said. "They like to change the furniture around a lot. I never know what it's going to look like in here when I get home."

Grace pretended to look at the fire. She tried to ignore Amy's smirk and the little pinch Amy gave her as she leaned over to pass her a dish of fruit. She wondered if Fiona had noticed Buddy's stains.

Amy looked up. "Tell us another story, Fiona. Like this morning."

Grace fished a little piece of cinnamon out of her dish and began to suck on it. She wasn't going to ask Fiona for any stories.

"The pirate," Amy said. "Tell us more about the pirate."

"You've been telling them about Grania O'Malley?" her father asked, smiling.

Fiona nodded. "I have."

"Did you tell them about Howth Castle?"

Fiona shook her head. "Would you like to hear . . ." she began.

"Yes," said Amy. She pushed at Grace's leg, but Grace didn't answer.

Fiona didn't say anything for a minute. Then she nodded again. "Granuaile O'Malley, it is then. The Pirate Queen. Well then . . . Grania had been traveling around in her ship . . ."

"The *White Sea Horse*," her father said.

"And she was tired and hungry. 'Find me a port,' she told her lookout. And he said, 'I see lights, and a castle on the shore.' So she sailed into port, thinking about the feast they'd give her for dinner."

Grace glanced at her father. He was leaning back in his chair, watching the fire. He still had a little smile on his face.

"And then . . ." Amy said.

"And then," said Fiona, "when she tried to get into the castle, the gates were locked. 'Let me in,' she told the gatekeeper, her eyes flashing. 'Oh, no,' said he. 'The lord is at his dinner and he will not be disturbed.' "

Fiona leaned over and touched Grace's head. "Now

Grace will understand that a pirate queen is brave and bold and will not take no for an answer."

Grace looked up at Fiona, then down again quickly.

"What did she do?" Amy asked.

"Well, the lord's little son was playing just outside the gates," Fiona said. "Grace thought for a moment. Then, quick as a wink, she scooped him up in her arms."

"Kidnapped him?" Grace asked, before she thought.

"To be sure," Fiona said. "She took him straight back to her ship."

"Terrible," Grace said.

"She was a fierce one, all right," said Fiona. "She had to be even fiercer than most, I guess, in order to make the other pirates afraid of her."

"Did she kill him?" Grace asked.

"Not a bit of it. She took him back to her own castle and waited. And, of course, when the lord heard about it, he was worried to tears, he was, and so he went straight to Grania's castle."

"What did she say?" Grace asked.

" 'You want your son back?' she asked. 'Well, there's a condition, there is.'

"And the lord said, 'Anything. I'll do anything.'

" 'I want a place set,' said Grania, 'at your table. Every night. From now on.' "

Fiona leaned forward and patted Grace's arm. "To this day, four hundred years later, it is set that way in the castle at Howth. And someday we'll talk your father into taking us there for a visit. And I'll show you the castle, and the lord's table, and the place that is set for Grania O'Malley."

For a moment no one spoke. Grace leaned forward on her elbows and watched the fire dancing in the stone fireplace. She wondered what it must have been like to be so brave and fierce.

Then her father slapped his leg. "You still tell the best stories, Fiona," he said. "I remember how we used to love to hear them when we were young. Katie . . ."

Fiona nodded. "I've been wanting to ask you," she said, "about Katie."

Grace felt herself stiffen. Since that day in the spring, over a year ago, the day that Mrs. Hunt had come to school for her and Amy, no one had talked about what had happened. She felt as if she couldn't look at her father. She wondered if he was going to be angry at Fiona for asking.

He took a long time answering. And then when he did, he said something that surprised her. "She was as good as a gilly," he said to Fiona. "You know that."

Fiona closed her eyes. "I remember," she said. "I remember the salmon, and the rushing water, and she always knew just where to cast her line."

A gilly, thought Grace. What a strange word. But she didn't want to ask. She put her head down, staring at the rug so she could see all the little blue pieces of wool sticking up.

"It was the first of April," her father said. "The start of the trout season . . . the day that the fishermen put on their hip boots and jackets and get into the river, no matter how bad the weather is." Her father's voice slowed and stopped.

Grace took a quick look at him and saw that tears were coming down his cheeks, dropping from his chin onto his shirt.

She wanted to reach out and touch his foot, but everyone was so quiet that she was afraid to move.

Her father spoke again. "The children were in school," he said, "and I had the day off. Katie wanted to fish. 'A holiday,' she called it. We walked to the lake in the pouring rain, and beyond to the stream in the mountains."

Suddenly Amy stood up. "I have to do my homework," she said, her voice sounding loud in the quiet room. She went into the kitchen. Grace could hear her moving around, opening books, rustling pages.

She put her head down on the rug. She wished she could remember what her mother looked like. She tried to picture her walking down the road with her father, wearing hip boots, stepping into the river . . .

"She slipped on a rock," he said. "It never should have happened. She hit her head. The water was fast. She went underneath. By the time I got to her . . ."

Suddenly there was an odd sound in the room.

Grace looked up. It was her father, his face all

twisted and funny, and the sound was the sound of his crying. It was not like the kind of crying she and Amy did; the noise of it was hard, as if it hurt his throat.

It was the first time she had ever seen him cry.

After what seemed a long time, he stood up. He bent his head toward Fiona and kissed her cheek. Then he whispered, "Thank you," and went out of the living room and upstairs to his bedroom.

Grace waited a little, then she looked up at Fiona. "What's a gilly?"

Fiona wiped her eyes. "A gilly is a guide," she said, "a fishing guide . . . someone who fishes wonderfully well." She shook her head. "Sometimes things happen and afterward you can't imagine why. And no matter how you try you can't go back and do them over."

Grace thought of her mother and then the bell. She nodded.

Fiona stood up. "It's bedtime, I'm thinking, macushla."

Grace stood up too.

Fiona reached out and patted her shoulder. "Your father had a right to cry. He needed it. Don't ever be foolish enough to think that has anything to do with not being brave."

Grace ducked her head. Then suddenly she reached up and kissed Fiona just as her father had done.

13

"Shaving cream for Daddy up in the closet, Amy's under the bed, a puzzle for Bianca in the—"

"Are you crazy?" Amy asked. "Talking to yourself like that?" She leaned over and twisted the television knob. "What's the matter with this thing? It's always going up and down."

"I'm going over the Christmas presents I have. But I still don't have enough money. Can you lend me a little?"

Amy banged on the television. "Can you pay me back before Christmas?"

"Uh . . . I don't think so," Grace said.

"Let's see. I have Daddy's. And Mrs. Gold's. I still have to get something for you. And Fiona." She looked up at the ceiling. "Four and two . . ." She shook her head. "I wish I could but . . ."

Grace swallowed. "Don't worry," she began, and broke off. "Fiona? I never thought of a present for Fiona."

"Of course." Amy reached into her pocket. "Want some?"

"What is it? Candy?"

"Ssh. Don't let Daddy hear you. I think he's right in the kitchen talking to Fiona."

"Why are you doing that?"

"Do you want some or not?" Amy slid half a Hershey bar across the rug toward her.

"You're going to get sick. Really sick. Don't you remember how you felt before we knew you had diabetes? Remember how thirsty you were all the time? And how tired?"

"What are you? Some kind of a doctor?" Amy banged the top of the television set again. "If you don't want it, don't take it."

Grace broke off a piece of chocolate, put it in her mouth, then closed her notebook.

Amy didn't answer. She kept looking at the television, her mouth closed in a tight line.

Grace stood up and went to the window. Outside, the snow had stopped. It was almost dark. Everything looked cold and empty; their front yard, Mr. Hunt's field. She could see a tiny pinprick of light moving back and forth on the opposite side of the field. It was probably Mr. Hunt's lantern. He must be outside feeding his goats. She tried to think of something to say to Amy, something that would make Amy do what she was supposed to do. She was so tired of nagging.

Fiona came to the living-room door, drying her hands on a dish towel. "It's time to eat, girls."

Grace shivered. She could feel the cold air coming through the sides of the window. She'd have to leave the garage door open a little tonight. When it was really cold, Buddy would sleep in there, curled up on some of Willie's leftover hay or on the old rag rug.

"What's for dinner?" Amy asked as they followed Fiona back into the kitchen.

"A pot meal," Fiona said. "Stew, nice and thick. It's the night for it."

Their father was at the table waiting for them. "What have you two been up to?" he asked, smiling.

"Homework," Amy said. "I have to write a paragraph on what I want for Christmas."

"That's nice," Fiona said. "And what is it you want?"

Amy looked up at the ceiling. "A shirt with fringe, I guess. Everybody has one. And some coins for my collection." She picked up her spoon. "Lots of stuff. Surprises."

"And you, Grania?" Fiona asked.

Grace sighed. What she really wanted was to go back to last Friday. She wouldn't have touched Mrs. Raphael's bell. She might have looked at it there on her desk for a minute. But then she would have grabbed up her social studies book and come right home. And she wished that Amy didn't have diabetes. But most of all she wished she could be like Amy, or the first Grania, afraid of nothing. Ready to . . .

"Well, is it so hard to think of something?" her father asked.

"Money," she burst out. "Could I do some work . . . earn some money?"

"Good idea," her father said. "Maybe you could help Fiona a little. Cooking . . . or cleaning up?"

"I will." Grace nodded. "But listen, Daddy, I've got to get to Binghamton. To the big mall for presents."

"I'm really sorry, Grace." He shook his head. "You'll have to make do with what you can find up on the highway. Try Sullivan's maybe. I have to go back to work every night until Christmas."

"And what do you think is wrong with me that I'm not to be trusted on American highways?" Fiona asked. "I drove a car over the muddiest roads in Ireland."

Amy began to giggle. Grace looked at her, knowing just what she was thinking.

Fiona knew too. "Just because my one eye is half-way to next week doesn't mean I can't see just as well with the other."

"I didn't mean . . ." Amy began.

Fiona waved her hand in the air. "Don't you be

worrying about it. It doesn't bother me one bit." She turned to their father. "Well, what about it, Fenton, are you going to lend me the car?"

He threw up his hands and laughed. "The car is here most of the time anyway. I like to walk to work."

Fiona nodded at them. "We'll have a grand time now, won't we, girls?"

Grace smiled across the table at her. Suddenly it was as if a weight had lifted off her chest. She'd find the bell, buy it, and put it on Mrs. Raphael's desk where it belonged. "I'll begin to earn money right now," she said. "I'll do the dishes while Fiona gets ready."

"We'll make it a grand Christmas too," Fiona said. "I'll start to bake tomorrow. I'll teach the girls to make brack. After all, we don't have much time. Christmas is a week from Tuesday."

"Brack?" Grace asked.

"Fruitcake, love," Fiona answered. "And we'll make cookies too. We'll leave the sugar out."

Grace's father ran his hand over his head. "Keep spoiling us, Fiona, and we'll never let you go home again."

Suddenly everything was still. Grace looked up at Fiona. It seemed as if she had been there forever. It looked as if she belonged there. Well, why not? a little voice inside her asked. Fiona loved them. And even her mother's ivy had the tiniest green shoot starting out of one side.

Her mother.

"We'll have to get a great tree for the living room," Fiona was saying.

"We always have a big tree," Grace said. "Up to the ceiling."

Fiona nodded. "That's good. I'll make popcorn with you and we'll string it all over the place."

Grace looked down at her stew. "We've never had any popcorn on the tree before. My mother always had just ornaments," she said, thinking she really didn't remember whether her mother had popcorn or not. She could tell her father and Amy were looking at her. They knew she was being mean.

She wondered what Fiona thought. She sneaked a quick look at her from under her eyelashes.

But Fiona didn't seem to mind at all. She was nodding across the table at Grace. "Good girl to be telling me." She turned to Amy. "I told you this girl was bold like the Pirate Queen." She nodded again. "I want to do everything the way it's always been done here. I want everything to be just right."

Grace picked up her roll again and took a small bite. Somehow it had lost its taste. She didn't want Fiona there. She didn't want her to keep trying and trying to do things right. She just wanted her to go away.

14

Fiona was a terrible driver. She knocked a small branch off the andromeda bush as she pulled out of the driveway. On Route 17 she drove so far over on the right side of the road that Grace could hear the sound of the gravel crunching under the wheels.

Grace and Amy sat in the back trying not to laugh.

"It's not me eye, my girls," Fiona told them. "Everything is backwards in America. The wheel is on the wrong side of the car and the drivers are on the wrong side of the road."

She looked at them through the rearview mirror and laughed. "It's never the Irish that are wrong."

"It's a good thing the highway is one way," Amy said. "Otherwise: whacko!"

"I'm learning," Fiona said. "Don't worry."

"I'm not," Amy said. "I never worry." She leaned forward. "Tell us a story."

"Don't you think I'd better watch my driving?"

"Do both," Amy said. "Tell me, were there any queens named Amy?"

"Certainly," Fiona said. "A princess. She had dark hair and blue eyes. She was a beautiful princess and everyone loved her. She liked to think about happy things."

"Where did she live? In a castle?" Amy asked.

Fiona laughed. "Well, some might call it a castle. A warm cozy castle."

Grace felt herself beginning to smile.

"The castle had a goat," Fiona said.

Amy started to laugh. "You mean me. I'm the princess." She looked at Grace, her eyes sparkling.

Grace squeezed her hand, then glanced out the window. "Here, Fiona, you have to turn here."

Fiona made a right turn, tires screeching, and pulled into the parking lot at the mall. She beat out a teen-age boy with long hair who was trying to get into the last space.

"Bundle up," Fiona said. "The wind will tear the clothes right off your back." She leaned out the door and waved to the boy, who was beeping at her. "I think there's another space down at the end," she called to him, ignoring the faces he was making.

The wind pulled at Grace's scarf and took her breath away as they hurried into the mall.

Inside, the mall looked like fairyland. There was a huge Christmas tree in the center covered with red and blue and yellow lights. Off to one side was a Santa Claus booth with little painted elves and reindeer outside and a line of children waiting to go in to see Santa.

Grace reached into her pocket and clutched her money tightly in her hand, her own four dollars, the money her father had given her to spend, and even a couple of dimes she had found in one of her sweater pockets.

She was glad they had left the garage doors open. By now Buddy would be nestled in the corner fast asleep on some hay.

Grace yawned. It was a good thing she had finished her homework before supper. By the time they got home, it would be past their bedtime and she still had to go out and make sure that Willie had enough water and hay for the night.

"I think we'd better separate," Amy said. "I don't want anyone to see what I'm getting."

"Good idea," Grace said.

"Are you sure you won't get lost?" Fiona asked, looking around. "This is a devilish big place."

"We always walk around by ourselves," Grace said.

Amy nodded. "Grace is right. We can meet by the fountain in about an hour."

Fiona glanced down the length of the mall doubt-fully. "Well, if you're sure . . ."

Grace didn't wait to hear the rest. She waved over her shoulder and hurried away.

A few seconds later she looked back. Amy was stand-ing in front of the record store. Her feet were tapping in time to the music.

Grace grinned to herself. Amy bought her a record every year. She probably would this year too.

Then she spotted Fiona. She was sitting on a bench next to the fountain watching the people walk by. Her head was turned to one side and she was smiling a little.

As Grace watched, a little girl with a balloon went up to Fiona and said something. They must have been talking about how pretty the fountain was because Fiona was pointing.

Suddenly the little girl let go of the balloon string. As it sailed away, Fiona reached up awkwardly and jumped for it.

She looked old enough to be a grandmother, Grace thought. She wondered why Fiona never bothered to fix her hair.

Then Fiona bent down and tied the string around the little girl's wrist. Her head was bent, but Grace could see that she was laughing. And just for a moment Fiona looked beautiful.

How silly. Fiona beautiful. Grace shook herself.

She'd have to hurry. The china shop was all the way down at the end and around the corner of the mall. She began to run.

As she turned the corner, she could see the shop window. It was filled with Christmas dishes and bowls. She stopped to see if she could find the bell, but it wasn't there. She felt a little edge of worry. Suppose it wasn't in the store? Suppose Lisa had made the whole thing up?

She opened the door and went inside. There must have been a million glasses and figurines on the counters. The aisles were crowded with people.

She looked around, trying to decide where to begin. Then she started for the aisle nearest the wall. Threading her way through the shoppers, she looked at everything carefully. By the time she reached the middle aisle she was sure she wasn't going to find it. Why, she wondered, would Lisa be so mean?

Then she saw it. It was up on a top shelf. She stood on tiptoes trying to be sure it was the same. She could just about see the little pink angel with the outspread wings. It had to be the same one.

"Hello, Grace," a voice said behind her.

She spun around. Bianca. She could feel the heat creeping up from her neck into her face.

Bianca smiled. "Getting Christmas presents?"

Grace nodded. She wondered if Bianca could see the

angel up on the shelf. Maybe if she started to walk a little bit. . . . "Have you found anything?" she asked, edging her way down the aisle.

Bianca shook her head. "I guess I'm going over to Family's. I'm just waiting for my mother. She's in line to get some dishes wrapped."

"Oh." Grace wondered what time it was. Suppose Bianca stood there talking to her for another twenty minutes? Suppose someone came along and tried to buy the bell? Maybe it was the last one.

"Well," Grace said, looking back over her shoulder a little. "It's pretty crowded tonight."

"Everyone's getting ready for Christmas," Bianca agreed. "Did you get anything for Mrs. Raphael yet?"

Grace shook her head. "Not yet."

"My mother's going to help me. I think we're going to buy her a scarf. I saw a really nice one . . ." She broke off. "There's my mother at the cash register. I have to go."

Grace watched her start down the aisle. Then Bianca turned back. "Don't get a scarf for her, all right?" She smiled and then she was gone.

Grace took a deep breath. She went back and looked at the bell again, then she went to the front of the store and waited at the counter until the clerk was finished.

"Can you help me?" she asked.

The clerk looked up.

"The bell in the back. With the angel? Can you tell me how much . . ."

The clerk followed her to the back of the store and stood on tiptoes. "Eight fifty-eight," she said. "Plus tax."

"How much tax?"

The clerk looked up at the ceiling. She had gum in her mouth. She chewed as she added everything up. "Sixty cents," she said finally.

"I'll take it."

She watched the clerk stand up on tiptoes again and reach for the bell, worried that she might drop it. But after a moment of fumbling the clerk took it gently off the top shelf and held it out to Grace.

"It's a little dusty," she said, "but I can clean it up for you. All right?"

Grace looked at the bell carefully. The same. Exactly the same one. She touched the angel's head with one finger. It was like a miracle. "Please. When you dust it," she said to the clerk. "Be careful."

The clerk clicked her gum. "I do this all the time. Never broke anything yet."

She followed the clerk to the front, feeling safe for the first time this week. She reached into her pocket and pulled out the crumpled bills. Then she added one of the dimes.

Enough. More than enough.

She looked up at the clerk.

The clerk nodded. She put the bell into a box and

wadded some tissue around it. "Looks good," she told Grace. "Doesn't it?"

She tore a sheet of Christmas paper off a roll. "I'll gift-wrap it. Right?"

Grace cleared her throat. "I guess so."

She watched as the clerk wrapped the box in red-and-green-striped paper.

It was too bad, she thought, that she'd have to take the paper off. It looked as if it would have been a beautiful Christmas present for someone.

She took the package and her change and went out the door and back down the mall. She stopped for a moment to look in one of the store windows. There was a little village scene with snow and tiny houses and a train chugging around and around. It was strange that she didn't feel happier. Now that she had the bell, everything should be all right. But still she had a nagging feeling of worry that she couldn't put her finger on.

15

While Grace did her work the next morning, she kept glancing over toward Mrs. Raphael's Christmas tree. The pile of packages under it grew larger every day.

There were only a few days left before Christmas vacation and she didn't have enough money for a decent present for Mrs. Raphael. She had spent almost all of it on the bell.

She thought about asking her father for more, but she had heard him saying something to Fiona the day before about how responsible she was and careful with money.

Responsible. She sighed. Don't think about it, she told herself. There's nothing you can do about it.

She looked over at Lisa Kile. As usual the kids had pulled their desks away from her. She sat in her island reading a storybook instead of doing her work.

She wondered why Lisa wasn't going to give Mrs. Raphael a present. Was it really because she didn't like her?

She shivered and thought about putting the bell back on Mrs. Raphael's desk. She had been afraid to bring it to school this morning . . . afraid that someone would see. This afternoon after everyone had gone home, she'd come back with it.

She could just see Mrs. Raphael when she came into school tomorrow morning and spotted it. She'd pick it up and look at it carefully to make sure it was all right, then she'd smile at the class.

But when she opened her presents . . . wouldn't she wonder why Grace didn't have a present for her? Yes. She'd wonder. She'd think Grace didn't like her. Maybe she could make a card. A special card. She had half a box of glitter upstairs in her dresser drawer left over from a project she had done last year.

As Grace opened the back door after school, Fiona was sitting in the kitchen knitting. She was going so fast with the needles that it reminded Grace of the *click, click, click* the Amtrak train made when it crossed the highway every night.

As Grace slammed the door behind her, Fiona jumped up and stuck the knitting behind her under the cushion.

Grace pretended she didn't notice the thick white

wool peeking out of the edge of the chair. Fiona must be making her a sweater for Christmas.

There was a plate of scones on the table. They looked like little brown castles. She sat down and took one.

"Butter, macushla," Fiona said. "It tastes better that way." She stood up and took a stick from the refrigerator. "This is my happiest Christmas," she said, as she put the butter on the table, "and you have made it so."

Grace looked up at her. "Why?"

"I never had my own house to fuss over," she said, "or children to love. And now I have both. Even if it's just for a little while."

Grace sat back. She didn't know what to say. She looked at Fiona's broad face and the gray frizzy hair and the eye that stared off into the distance. It was funny that when Fiona talked, it was hard to remember that she wasn't pretty. She had such a nice, soft voice.

"Fiona," Grace said. "Can I ask you something?"

Fiona sat down next to her and cocked her head.

"If you were a teacher . . ."

Fiona leaned forward a little. "Yes?"

"Suppose a kid made a card for you instead of giving a present. A really special card. Maybe with glitter stuff on it."

"I'd love it," Fiona said. "I'd treasure it always. I'd

put it on my dresser and look at it every day and think about the little girl who made me such a nice thing, I would."

Grace took another scone. She wondered how Mrs. Raphael would feel about getting a card instead of a present. She thought about it while she finished the scone. Maybe if she made the card really wonderful . . .

She stood up. That's what she'd do.

"I wanted to tell you," Fiona said, "that devil of a dog was back today." She ran her hand over her hair. "He's a big one, and fierce. I saw him over near your goat's pen. He'd probably like to rip her to pieces."

Grace tried not to smile. Willie and Buddy were friends. In the summertime they'd run around the yard, and Willie would pretend to butt the dog, and Buddy would growl and bark . . .

"But worse than that, Grania, I'm worried about you. Suppose that dog goes after you. . . ." Fiona shuddered. "His long teeth. I can see them now, ripping into—" She broke off. "It's too awful to think about."

Grace stood up. "Why are you so worried about dogs all the time?"

Fiona turned back to the counter. "I'm not like Grace O'Malley, the pirate," she said. "I'm afraid of those beasts."

"That dog wouldn't hurt anyone," Grace said. "I was just teasing you."

Fiona shook her head. "You're a brave girl," she said. "Brave as a sword."

Grace looked over at her. A little beam of light had caught the reflection of the cracked vase on the windowsill. It played across Fiona's frizzy hair, making it look like a slice of purple rainbow.

"Brave like Grace O'Malley?" Grace asked, smiling.

"Yes," Fiona said, "you're like Grace. I was thinking about that before, reminding myself to tell you another story I remember about her."

Grace sat on the edge of the table. She should really go upstairs and work on the card. But she thought about the pirate and her ship and the red dress she wore. "Go ahead," she told Fiona.

"You've heard of Queen Elizabeth? The English queen in the 1500s?"

Grace nodded.

"She was a strong queen, with her red hair and her straight back, and she wanted to see for herself this pirate woman who ruled the west coast of Ireland." Fiona leaned forward. "So she asked Grace O'Malley to visit her."

"Did she go?"

"She did. Some people say she went in the green robes of an Irish chieftain. And Queen Elizabeth thought she was so wonderful that she told Grace she'd make her a countess."

"Countess Grania," Grace said.

"Not a bit of it. Grace drew herself up taller than the queen and said, 'I am a queen in my own land, equal to you.'"

Grace felt as if she could almost see her, standing in the bright green robe, brave and sure of herself. She wondered if she really looked like her. She wished she had a chief's robe to wear, to wrap around herself so she'd feel brave. She'd have a hood and cover her whole head, except for her eyes, and go to Mrs. Raphael and tell her the truth. She swallowed. Instead she'd take the bell to Mrs. Raphael's desk later and she'd bring a beautiful card with her. She'd make a lovely tree, green like the robe of Grace O'Malley, and draw sparkly gold presents underneath.

"I'm going upstairs, Fiona," she said, "to make a card for my teacher."

"Why don't you work on it in here," Fiona said, "or in the living room? Amy's upstairs sleeping."

Grace frowned. She could feel her heart give a little skip. "Is she sick?"

Fiona shook her head. "She said she wasn't. She said she just wanted to take a little nap."

Grace nodded. "All right. I'll tiptoe upstairs and get my stuff. Then I can spread everything out on the floor."

A few minutes later she put a piece of creamy white

drawing paper and the box of glitter on the living-room floor. Then she sat and looked at the paper, measuring it in her mind.

Finally she picked up a pencil and began to draw a tree.

16

The card just wouldn't come out the way Grace wanted it to. She could see the tree just as plain as anything in her mind, but it didn't look like that on the paper.

It took her half a package of paper and most of the afternoon to finish. Then she went into the kitchen to show Fiona.

"Perfect," Fiona said, "and look at the presents under the tree. They sparkle like the sun on a river." She gave Grace a hug. "Your teacher will love it."

Grace looked at the card again. She hoped Fiona was right.

She took a brown paper bag out of the drawer, then went upstairs and put the red-and-green bell package and the card in it.

Five minutes later she was back at school. There was

no one on the second floor. Mike, the custodian, had already been there. The desks were back in their neat rows and Lisa Kile's island was gone.

She went over to the tree and leaned forward to sniff at the branches. They smelled sweet and fresh, like the pine forest in the summertime. There were so many presents that they didn't all fit on the table. Four or five were stacked underneath on the floor.

Grace tried to decide which one was the prettiest. There was a green package on the top with a gold star in the middle instead of a bow. The star was a little crooked. It looked as if someone had cut it out of shiny paper and glued it on herself.

Under the green one there was a long flat package. She pulled it out to get a better look. It was blue, just the color of Mrs. Raphael's eyes, and had a lot of silver glitter all over it. She wondered what was in it, but even though she shook it gently, it didn't make any noise.

She turned the tag over. It was Bianca's. A scarf.

She brought her card over to the table and propped it up against the bottom of the tree. Then she stood back to look at it.

Somehow, one of the edges of the card had gotten wrinkled. The tall green tree she had drawn so carefully looked a little as if it would fall over if someone gave it a poke, and the glittering presents underneath looked lopsided.

She should have known better than to ask Fiona.

She sighed and pushed the card underneath one of the packages.

She reached into the brown paper bag and pulled out the box with the bell in it. She arranged the red bow with the loops sticking up just right. It was a shame to tear open the paper and take it out.

Why couldn't she just give it to the teacher herself? Put her name on it and . . .

She ran her hand gently over the ribbon. Wrong. It would be wrong. To break someone's bell and then pretend to give her a new one for Christmas. Mrs. Raphael would hold up the bell for the class to see. "What a thoughtful child," she'd say. And she'd have to sit there and pretend that she'd never had anything to do with starting the whole thing.

She looked down at the table. Lisa Kile's card was lying in the corner. She had used a piece of looseleaf folded in half and had written on the front in brown crayon: "Merry Christmas to the Teacher."

No wonder Mrs. Raphael didn't like her. It looked as if Lisa didn't care about anything.

Grace took the end of the ribbon on the box and started to pull it.

Suppose?

Yes, suppose she put Lisa's name on it? Then Mrs. Raphael would think Lisa had bought it to replace the broken one.

She wondered whether anyone had ever done anything nice for Lisa. She remembered Lisa running down the steps of the tower, coming back with the candy for Amy. What would Grace have done if Lisa hadn't been there?

"All right," she said out loud. "I owe you."

Slowly she put the bell package under the tree. She picked up the looseleaf card Lisa had made and tried to tuck it under the red ribbon.

If Mrs. Raphael thought that Lisa had brought the bell, she might be different toward her. Lisa might not have to sit in an island anymore. The kids would see that Mrs. Raphael was being nice to her and maybe they'd be nicer too.

Grace pushed the card under the ribbon a little more, but it wouldn't stay. She went back to her desk for her pen. Then she put the card under the box and carefully wrote on the red-and-green-striped paper: "From Lisa." She made a big loopy *L* just the way Lisa always did.

Outside, she was surprised how good she felt. Even though she didn't have a present for the teacher, she was beginning to have the feeling of Christmas inside.

Instead of going straight home, she decided she'd go up the lake road. It was snowing a little, but she didn't feel cold as she walked.

She looked at the lake from the side of the road. It was beginning to ice up and look like a Christmas card.

"Hey, Grace."

She looked up. It was Lisa.

"What are you doing here?"

Grace shrugged. "Just taking a walk."

Lisa came over to her. She had pulled her old purple hat on so that one of her ears was sticking out. "Feels like Christmas," she said.

"I was just thinking that," Grace answered.

"Did you do your Christmas shopping?"

"Some."

"I did too," Lisa said. "My mother even gave me money for a present for Mrs. Raphael."

Grace turned. "You bought the teacher a present?"

"Yeah." Lisa grinned. "I wasn't going to." She raised one shoulder. "But I did anyway. Yellow. My favorite color."

Grace stopped walking. "Listen," she said, "it's getting dark. I have to go back now."

"Want me to walk you down?"

"No." Grace waved and started back down the road. She wondered what Mrs. Raphael would say when she saw that Lisa had given her two presents. Wouldn't she think it was odd?

Maybe she'd better go back and take Lisa's name off that package. It had been a silly thing to do anyway.

She started to run.

By the time she reached the school, it was dark. The snow was swirling around the lights in the school yard.

She tried the door but it was locked. Then she ran around to the front. The doors there were locked too. She'd have to wait until morning. She'd have to get there before anyone else.

Slowly she walked out of the school yard. She stopped at the gate. How would Mrs. Raphael know it was a new bell? Suppose she thought that Lisa had stolen the bell and wrapped it up. Maybe she'd think it was just the kind of crazy thing that Lisa might do.

No. Mrs. Raphael wouldn't think that. Or would she?

She might. She would. Grace started for home. Her mouth felt dry. Why had she done it?

She let herself in the back door. Fiona was in the kitchen making dinner. She was singing an Irish song.

It was a song Grace loved. Usually it made her want to march around and clap her hands. But tonight she thought about the words.

"It's about the bravest of men," Fiona had said. "Irishmen." She'd put her hand on Grace's shoulder. "And it happened in front of the post office in Dublin way back in 1916. It was on an Easter Monday morning that one hundred fifty Irishmen in ragged uniforms stood under the green flag of Ireland. They said that Ireland would be free even if they died for it. And by the end of the day, a thousand Irishmen stood with them."

Fiona wiped her eyes. "And you know, Grania, they held off the mighty British soldiers for seven long days."

"What happened then?" Grace had asked, thinking that she never would have been brave enough to do such a thing.

"In the end," Fiona said, "the leaders were shot by the British." She nodded slowly. "But Ireland never forgot those brave men and it made her even more determined to be free."

Now Fiona stopped singing when she saw Grace in the doorway. She dried her hands on a towel. "Well, macushla," she said in her soft voice. "Did you bring the card to the classroom?"

Grace jerked her head up and down a couple of times and shrugged out of her jacket. She could feel Fiona looking at her as she hung the jacket on the kitchen hook.

Grace looked up at the mirror. There was a streak of dirt on her cheek, but otherwise it didn't look as if she had been crying. She rubbed at the mark and turned around.

Her father and Amy were at the table already. He was cutting thick slices of ham. Amy had her mouth full of Fiona's soda bread. Her father looked across at her and smiled.

"I don't feel well," she said. "I think I'd better go to bed."

As she started upstairs, she could hear Fiona saying she'd make her a cup of tea in a little while.

She lay in bed for a long time thinking about the bell, and the Irishmen in front of the post office, and Grania, the Pirate Queen.

Then she heard Fiona's heavy steps on the stairs. She pulled the covers halfway over her head and squeezed her eyes shut.

She heard the door open, and the sound of the cup and saucer as Fiona put the tea on the table. Fiona must have stood there for a moment, looking down at her, because she could hear her soft breathing. Then there were footsteps and the door closed behind her.

17

It was just about light when Grace jumped out of bed the next morning. Amy was still in a round lump under her quilt.

Grace padded over to look at her. Amy's face seemed red and puffy.

Grace reached out and pulled at her pajama sleeve. "Are you all right?"

Amy moved irritably under her hand. "Go away," she mumbled.

Grace grabbed her jeans and put them on as quickly as she could. Then she dashed downstairs. She had to be the first one in school.

She wasn't though. Even though she ate her breakfast standing up and ran all the way to Front Street, someone was there ahead of her.

It was Lisa Kile. She was playing hopscotch in the corner of the school yard by herself.

Grace backed away as she saw her, but it was too late. Lisa looked up. "Hey, Gracie," she yelled. "You're here early."

"I have to get something." She walked past Lisa and went to pull open the heavy doors.

"They're locked," Lisa called after her. "Mike doesn't open them for another ten minutes."

Grace pulled at the doors again as hard as she could. Lisa was right. She couldn't budge them.

She started for the side of the school. Maybe the auditorium doors . . .

"They're locked too," Lisa yelled. "Everything is. You can't get in."

"I've got to get in," she said, mumbling the words so Lisa couldn't hear her. She could feel the cold through her jacket. The wind swept sand and papers across the yard, stinging her eyes.

She huddled next to the door, shivering, and watched Lisa out of the corner of her eye.

Lisa had gone back to her hopscotch game. She was jumping around and it looked as if she was talking to herself.

A few minutes later a bunch of kids came into the yard. Lisa backed away from the game and stood against the wall.

Grace kept watching the doors, waiting for Mike. Finally he opened them. She raced inside and ran down the hall.

"You're not supposed to be in here until the bell rings," he yelled after her. He sounded grumpy.

Grace didn't answer him. She dashed upstairs to the classroom and turned the knob. But the door was locked too. She could feel her hands trembling.

She raced back downstairs to look for Mike.

He was in the custodian's room.

"Could you open . . ." she began, and had to stop to catch her breath. "The door to two seventeen is locked. I have to get in."

He shook his head. "Can't."

"Please," Grace said and started to cry.

For a moment he didn't say anything. Then he got up from his seat. "Well, I guess so. What did you do? Forget your homework or something?"

She nodded, trying not to sniffle. "Something."

She followed him up the stairs, wondering why he always walked so slowly. She felt like pulling the big bunch of keys out of his hands and running upstairs by herself.

She stopped at the top of the stairs. Mrs. Raphael was there ahead of her. She was standing at the classroom door with her keys in her hand.

"Good morning, Mike," she said. Then she spotted Grace. She blinked and looked down at her watch. "You're early, Grace."

"Yes," Grace said. She could hardly talk. Her mouth was so dry it felt as if her tongue was stuck to the roof of her mouth.

"Too early," Mrs. Raphael said. "Run along outside and wait for the bell." She turned to Mike. "As long as you're here, maybe you'll fix those shades for me."

Mike looked back at Grace. He shook his head.

Grace tiptoed down the stairs to the first floor and went into the girls' room. It was the one for the little kids. The first and second graders. There were no locks on the doors and the seats were so low they looked as if they were made for midgets.

Grace stood at the window and looked down at the school yard. There were a lot of kids out there now. She couldn't see Lisa Kile anymore, but some of the other kids in the class were playing hopscotch.

Finally the bell rang. She walked upstairs to her classroom and went to her seat. Before she sat down, she turned to look at the tree. The little green-and-red-striped package was there right in front.

All morning while she did her work, she kept looking over at it. Maybe during lunchtime she could come back and take the package away

But suppose Mrs. Raphael saw her with it?

Maybe she could just tear off the piece of paper with Lisa's name on it. She could tape the rest of it together somehow. Or just leave it torn. No one would know that she had done it.

She looked up at the big clock on the wall. It seemed to be 10:30 forever. She kept checking the red second hand to make sure it was still going. Finally it moved. An hour and fifteen minutes until lunchtime. Then an hour. Then fifteen minutes. Maybe she'd be lucky.

But she wasn't.

Just before lunch, when everyone was running around, looking for lunch bags, and coats, and baseball bats to take out to the yard, Mrs. Raphael went over to the tree.

She stood there for a moment looking down at the packages. She straightened them a little. Then she picked up a package wrapped in yellow.

What a funny color for a Christmas present, Grace thought.

Mrs. Raphael must have thought so too because she turned over the tag to see whose it was.

Lisa, thought Grace. She saw Mrs. Raphael look over toward Lisa, so she was probably right.

Mrs. Raphael put the yellow package down and touched the red and green one.

Grace felt her heart start to beat a little faster.

Mrs. Raphael looked over toward Lisa. "Two presents?" she asked.

Lisa was combing her hair through her fingers, looking out the window. She didn't even hear Mrs. Raphael.

"Lisa," said Mrs. Raphael sharply.

Lisa jumped.

"Two presents for me?" Mrs. Raphael asked again. She patted the yellow box.

Lisa looked as if she was trying to figure out what Mrs. Raphael was talking about. She shrugged a little, then she lowered her eyes and quickly pulled out her notebook and her pencil.

Mrs. Raphael turned back to the table.

Grace glanced over at Lisa.

Lisa looked back at her. She made a funny face and twirled her finger around her ear. "Crazy," she mouthed.

Mrs. Raphael spun around. "What did you say, Lisa?" She stared at Lisa angrily.

Lisa didn't answer. She looked down at her desk.

"Why did you say that?" Mrs. Raphael asked.

Lisa began to fiddle with her pencil.

"Lisa? I'm talking to you."

Lisa looked up slowly. "I don't know what you're talking about."

Mrs. Raphael sighed. "I was talking about the Christmas presents. The two packages."

Grace bit the inside of her lip. Andrew had his hand

up in the air, trying to get Mrs. Raphael's attention. Please, she thought, let Mrs. Raphael see him.

"I don't know about any two presents," Lisa said.

"This is yours?" Mrs. Raphael said, pointing to the yellow one.

Lisa nodded.

Andrew waved his hand harder. "Mrs. Raphael?"

Mrs. Raphael pointed to the red-and-green-striped package. "And this one too."

Lisa shook her head.

"Isn't this yours?" Mrs. Raphael picked it up. "It has your name on it."

"Not my name. I didn't write it."

Andrew took a ball out of his pocket. "We're going to be late for lunch," he said. "We'll never get out to recess."

"You wrote it," Mrs. Raphael said. "It has the same big loop for the *L*."

"No."

"Mrs. Raphael," Andrew said again.

Mrs. Raphael ran one of her fingernails under the red ribbon. It broke with a little popping sound. Then she tore off the paper and opened the box.

"My bell," she said. She looked up at Lisa.

Suddenly everyone was quiet.

Mrs. Raphael cleared her throat. "Why did you . . ."

"I didn't . . ." Lisa began, and stopped. She got that

look she always had when Mrs. Raphael was scolding her.

Mrs. Raphael stood there for another moment staring hard at Lisa. Then she turned to the class. "It's time for lunch," she said. "Line up, class."

18

Everything had gone back to normal after Mrs. Raphael put the bell back on her desk. At least it looked that way. They hurried downstairs for lunch and Mrs. Raphael didn't say one more word about what had happened while she waited for everyone to get settled in the cafeteria.

At the table Grace took one bite of her sandwich, but it tasted so dry that she could hardly swallow it. She threw it in the pail at the side of the counter and waited there until the monitor opened the doors to the school yard.

A few minutes later Bianca and some of the other kids came outside with the jump rope. "Come on, Grace," they yelled.

Usually she was one of the best jumpers. But this time she kept missing so she was an ender for most of the time. As the rope slapped hard against the cement, all the kids were yelling:

Mush. Mush. Walk on slush.
Jump the rope in a rush.

But underneath, Grace could hear: _tell, tell._ And then when the rope went really fast: _Pirate Queen, Pirate Queen._ She kept looking over toward the fence. Lisa was standing there, her back to the school yard. Grace wondered how she could stay there in the cold for so long without moving.

In class, all afternoon, she thought about going to Mrs. Raphael and telling her what really happened. But she knew she wouldn't.

Every time she looked at Lisa, Lisa was staring at the books on her desk. She never looked back at Grace. But she didn't seem any different from the way she usually did. Grace wondered what she was thinking. Did she remember telling Grace where the bell came from?

Grace was the first one out at dismissal. She crossed the street and hurried across the fields to her yard.

Willie was nibbling at some of the pellets in her tray when Grace opened the gate. Still chewing, the goat butted her gently.

Grace leaned against the fence and ran her hands

gently over Willie's head. Then Willie went back to her tray and Grace went across the yard to the kitchen. She knew Fiona would be waiting. Today was the day she was going to teach them how to make brack for Christmas.

Fiona looked up when she opened the door. "Is it you then?" she said. "Come in out of the cold."

Grace dropped her books on the bench. "Are we going to make brack?" she asked. She tried to make her voice sound excited. For three days Fiona had been telling them how happy she was to be teaching them Irish cooking.

But Fiona didn't seem happy now. Grace darted a quick look at her as she unzipped her jacket. The lines in Fiona's face looked a little deeper.

"What's the matter?" Grace asked.

"I'm worried about Amy," Fiona said.

Grace stopped with one arm out of her jacket. "Is she sick?"

"I don't know. I didn't like the look of her when she came in from school. All red in the face somehow. She said she was all right, though. She said she just wanted to lie down for a while."

"Not an insulin reaction?"

"No." Fiona shook her head. "It's not that. She didn't seem weak or shaky."

"What's the matter then?"

Fiona shook her head. "I don't know. She said she was sleepy. Maybe it's nothing."

"I'll go up." Grace pulled off her jacket and took the stairs two at a time.

At the door of the bedroom, she hesitated. Amy was curled up as usual on her side almost covered by the red and white quilt.

"Amy?" Grace whispered. She tiptoed over to the bed.

Amy didn't move. Her face was red and she was breathing loudly.

Grace shook her by the shoulder. "Wake up."

Amy made a little sound under her breath, but she didn't open her eyes.

Fiona was right. This wasn't like the insulin reactions Amy had when she didn't eat enough. Grace bent over her a little bit, looking at her. She ran her hand across Amy's face. Her skin was hot and dry.

Grace could feel the fear coming up in her throat. "Amy, wake up."

What was the matter with her?

Then she remembered Dr. Irving sitting next to the bed when Amy first had diabetes. "Like a pendulum," he had said. "When you have diabetes, you have to eat just right. Too little and you'll have an insulin reaction. Too much of the wrong food and you'll go into a diabetic coma."

Too much. Candy every day. Cookies. And maybe a lot of other things that Grace hadn't even seen.

She ran down the hall. From the top of the stairs she could hear Christmas music coming from the kitchen radio.

"Fiona," she yelled.

She waited a second, then raced down the stairs.

The outside door was open. Grace could see Fiona running across the yard. She was yelling something.

Grace didn't stop to hear what it was.

She picked up the little telephone book her father kept by the phone and turned to the *I*'s.

Then she dialed and waited to hear the voice of Dr. Irving's nurse.

"Fiona," she yelled as the phone rang. "Fiona."

"Grace," Fiona's voice came back. "Come help me. It's that devil."

"Dr. Irving's office."

"Please," Grace began. It was hard to get her breath. "I need to talk to Dr. Irving."

"Sorry," the nurse said. It sounded as if she was talking to someone in the office at the same time. "He's not here."

"My sister is sick," Grace said, "really sick."

"Dr. Irving just left. He should be back in an hour or two. If you'll leave your name and number . . ."

Quickly Grace gave them to her and hung up. She

wouldn't be able to wait that long for the doctor. She ran to the back door.

The wind was blowing across the yard, sending dried leaves and twigs up in little spirals. The gate to Willie's pen banged back and forth. She must have forgotten to lock it.

Willie was outside, chewing on a dead petunia plant.

Fiona, hair blowing across her face, stood at one corner of the pen trying to get the goat inside. Buddy was in her way. He darted around her, barking.

Grace could see that Fiona was terrified. "Devil," Fiona yelled at Buddy. She threw herself toward Willie and pulled her by one ripply horn.

"Let them be, Fiona," Grace yelled over Buddy's barking. "It's all right."

But Fiona didn't hear her. With one last tug she shoved Willie inside her pen and hooked the gate.

"Fiona," she called again.

This time Buddy heard her and bounded over. He circled around her once to say hello, then he raced out of the yard.

Fiona turned and saw her. "I did it, macushla," she said. There was a look of triumph on her face as she looked at Grace. "I saved the goat from that devil dog."

"Fiona, please," Grace said. "The car. Did Daddy walk to work today? We have to take Amy to the hospital."

Fiona stared at her for a second. "It's in the garage," she said. She began to move. She ran to the kitchen for the keys.

"If you bring the car to the front," Grace said, "I'll go up and get her ready. But I'll need help."

Fiona nodded once and went out the back door.

Upstairs, Amy was lying in the same spot. Grace pulled at her arm. "We've got to get you up," she said. Amy moaned a little and leaned against her.

Grace locked her arms around Amy and braced her legs against the bed. Then she heaved Amy up into a sitting position.

Amy, who always looked so little and skinny, was heavier than she thought. It was hard to swing her legs over the side of the bed and get her up on her feet.

By that time Fiona was back. Together they wrapped the quilt around Amy and guided her downstairs and out to the car.

Grace kept talking to Amy as she held her in the backseat of the old car. She pushed Amy's dark hair away from her face and told Fiona how to find the hospital.

It seemed to take a long time to get there. And by the time they reached the circular driveway to the hospital, Grace felt as if they had been driving forever. She couldn't wait to get Amy inside and get help.

19

A nurse whisked Amy away from them and pointed to a door. "Wait in there," she said. "I'll be back to tell you what's going on as soon as I can."

The little tan waiting room was decorated for Christmas. A tree shimmering with tinsel stood in one corner and bunches of Christmas cards hung on a bulletin board. Grace sat there staring at them for a long time.

Then Fiona patted her hand. "She'll be all right, I'm sure, and it's all because of you."

Grace shook her head.

"It is true, you know," Fiona said. "You did everything just right."

Grace made a sound in her throat. She wondered what Fiona would think if she really knew how she did things, if she knew what a coward she was to have broken the bell and let Lisa Kile get the blame for it.

She stood up and went over to the window. It had started to snow. Already the cars in the parking lot were covered with a thin white blanket. Her father would be coming home from work soon.

Her father . . .

"Fiona," she said. "We forgot to call Daddy."

Fiona pulled herself to her feet. "Glory. I forgot all about him. I'll go down the hall and find a phone."

Grace looked out the window again. Suppose Amy died?

There'd be no one upstairs in the bed next to her at night. No Amy to climb the fire tower with her.

She thought of the summer, the hot days when she and Amy would take their bikes up to the picnic grove and eat their sandwiches in the shade.

Would she forget what Amy looked like in a couple of months the way she had with her mother? She tried to picture Amy's face. Even now it was hard to think of what she looked like.

Behind her there was a step. She whirled around. It was Dr. Irving.

He smiled at her. "It was lucky I stopped at the hospital on my way home."

"Is she going to die?"

He shook his head. "No. She's feeling a little better

now. We gave her some insulin and we're feeding her through a tube in her arm." He sighed. "We'll have to keep her here a few days and try to get her back on her diet."

Grace let out her breath. She could feel her legs begin to shake a little. She pressed her hands together. They were freezing.

The doctor put his arm on her shoulder. "I'll let you see her for a few minutes."

She nodded and followed him out into the hall. Fiona was nowhere in sight.

"What about Fiona?" she asked the doctor.

"Who's Fiona?"

"She's my . . . our . . ." Grace hesitated. "She takes care of us."

"The nurse will tell her where you are."

He led her to a small room at the end of the corridor.

"Just stay for a few minutes," he said. "I'll be down at the end of the hall at the nurses' station."

Grace tiptoed into the room and looked at Amy. Her face was still red and her eyes were closed. There was a small white bandage on her arm. A long plastic tube snaked out of the bandage and up to a large bottle on a stand.

"I love you, Amy," she whispered in a voice so low her lips barely moved.

Amy's eyes flew open. She grinned. "Hey, Gracie,"

she said in a whispery voice, "did you bring me a box of candy?"

Grace went toward the bed. "Don't."

"Just joking."

"Don't joke."

Amy's eyes opened a little wider. "Are you mad at me?"

Grace shook her head. Then suddenly she nodded. She could feel the anger in her chest and even in her throat. "Do you want to die?" she asked. "And all for some candy and some pieces of cake?"

Amy shook her head impatiently. "You're always yelling about that."

"Why don't you do what you're supposed to do? You're making me afraid all the time," she said, the words feeling hard and hurting her throat. She took a step away from the bed. "I hate you, Amy. I hate you."

In back of her she felt hands on her shoulders. "Grania," Fiona said in a soft voice.

But she whirled away from Fiona's hands and out the door. She ran down the corridor, past the nurses' station. She saw Dr. Irving take a step toward her but she didn't pay any attention to him.

She rushed through the front doors of the hospital and out into the snowy parking lot. She wrenched open the door to the car and climbed in the front seat.

She was shivering and her throat felt sore. She wondered why she wasn't crying. She wondered how she could have said such a terrible thing to Amy.

A few minutes later she heard Fiona's footsteps. Fiona opened the door on the driver's side and slid in next to her.

"Now," she said to Grace, "it's home we'll be going. Amy's good and safe where she is, and it's us who'll be needing a hot cup of tea and something soft that will slip down easy and comfort us." She started the car. "It's way past dinner time and your father will stop at the hospital on his way home."

After a moment Fiona began to sing. Grace half listened as she sang about dancing and the sound of Irish bagpipes on a summer evening. The car began to warm up, and suddenly Grace began to feel sleepy. Her eyes kept closing and it was an effort to look out of the window into the darkness. She found herself sliding over closer to Fiona and leaning against her soft arm.

"We're home," Fiona said after a while. "Wake up now and come into the house."

Grace stumbled out of the car and up the back steps into the kitchen. "I have to feed my goat," she told Fiona, yawning. She filled the pan with pellets as Fiona took butter and eggs out of the refrigerator. "I'll be back in a minute."

Outside, she went across the yard in the darkness. She could see that Willie wasn't in the front part of her pen. It was late. Maybe she was asleep already. Grace banged the edge of the pan against the gate but it was too cold to wait for Willie to come out. She slid the pan under the chicken wire and went back into the house. She wished she could tell Amy that she hadn't meant what she said. She couldn't wait to finish dinner so she could go upstairs to bed.

20

It was just starting to get light when Grace opened her eyes. She had dreamed of Amy. She wondered if Amy was homesick. Maybe she was awake and thinking about what she had said to her last night.

If only she hadn't said it. If only she could see Amy right now for one minute to tell her she didn't mean it.

She slid her legs out of the blankets and went over to the window. It was still snowing a little. Lisa said she got up early every morning. Was she outside somewhere in the snow thinking about yesterday too?

She crossed her arms over her chest and shivered. She wondered if she would ever feel like herself. Just Grace. Not having to worry about Amy or having gotten Lisa into such trouble.

She looked down at the yard. There were large paw

prints all over. Buddy must have been there looking for breakfast. The snow in front of Willie's pen was smooth and even, though. Willie hadn't been out yet.

Willie was usually the first one up. Maybe she'd better go downstairs and take a look. She threw on her robe and went to the stairs. She could hear her father moving around in his bedroom, getting ready for work.

Downstairs, Fiona was in the kitchen. She was sitting in the chair, knitting. This time the wool was dark blue. She held the needles up for Grace to see. "A hat for your father," she said, "to cover his poor bald spot."

Grace smiled. She'd have to tell Amy . . . "I have to go out and check on Willie," she said.

"No coat?" Fiona asked. "No boots?"

"Boots. There are some by the stairs. I'll just slip them on and run out. I don't know why . . ." she began, thinking about Willie. "I'll take her some water first."

Outside, the wind was blowing around the corner of the house, and the snow had drifted up on one side of the yard. It would be a great place for a fort if Amy had been there.

She crossed the yard to the pen and opened the chicken-wire gate. "Willie?" she called.

From inside the shed she heard the soft sound Willie made when she answered her.

"Come on out here, I'm freezing." She set the water pan down, then waited. "Willie?"

Slowly she went into the shed. It was still almost dark inside, and warmer, the sides of the walls and the floor piled high with hay.

"What's the matter with you?" Grace asked, moving closer to her.

Willie blinked slowly, covering her pale green eyes with her fringed lashes for a moment.

"What's the matter?" Grace asked again. She could hear Buddy outside now, barking. He was probably hungry too. She'd have to bring something out to him.

Then she saw something move. Almost the color of the hay, darker than Willie. Nestled against her side. One . . . no, two. Long and leggy. Twins.

"How . . ." she began, as she knelt down in the hay and touched them gently. "I didn't even know," she said. The larger twin raised his head, looking exactly like Mr. Hunt's goat, Ralph.

"Wait till Amy . . ." she said. "And even Lisa . . ." Lisa would love to see . . .

She shook her head and stood up. "I'll get you something to eat, Willie," she said, "and bring your water inside."

She stopped in the yard to give Buddy a pat, then yelled for Fiona. "Babies, Fiona."

Fiona opened the back door. "The goat?"

Grace went into the kitchen, stamping snow off her boots. "It's freezing out there. Yes. Twins."

"That little round goat," Fiona said, "hiding such a secret. You'll have to help her with names."

Grace nodded. "Amy can name one of them." She poured pellets into Willie's pan. "I've got to hurry. Get dressed as soon as I feed her." She turned back to Fiona. "Wait till Daddy sees them." She opened the refrigerator door. "I've got to take a little hamburger meat."

"Goats eat . . . ?" Fiona began.

Grace shook her head. "It's that dog, Fiona. Buddy. It's cold out there. He's hungry." She looked up at Fiona. "Please?"

Fiona nodded slowly. "You're a one," she said. "Take it, of course."

Grace opened the back door. Buddy was standing at the bottom of the steps, wagging his tail at her. She threw him the meat and watched as he ate it down in one gulp. Then as she shut the door, he turned and raced out of the yard.

Behind her, her father touched her head. "How are you today?" he asked.

She twirled around. "You'll never guess what happened. Willie had twins." She pulled him by the hand. "Come and look. You'll love them."

He pulled his jacket off the chair and shrugged into it.

"Want to come, Fiona?" Grace asked.

"Go along with your dad," Fiona said. "I'll stay here and mind the pancakes."

Grace picked up Willie's dish and walked with her father across the yard. When they got to the shed, she sank down next to the baby goats while Willie ate.

Her father leaned against the shed wall. "Fiona said you were wonderful about getting Amy to the hospital," he said. "Brave."

She ducked her head down. "I'm not."

"I think you were." He bent down to look at the goats. "I saw Amy last night."

"She's better?"

"Yes. And she had a message for you. She said there's something she wants you to know. She said it's hard to stay on that diet every day. Really hard. And sometimes she tries to pretend that she doesn't have diabetes."

He shook his head slowly. "I understand that," he said. "Until Fiona came, I never wanted to talk about your mother. I guess I thought if I didn't talk about her, it would seem as if she were still here. In the kitchen maybe, or up at the lake, fishing."

Grace could almost see her mother standing at the

shallow end of the lake, the wind whipping her long dark hair across her face. "I wish she was here."

"Sometimes, Gracie, she is here. In our hearts, in what we remember of her." He reached out and rubbed the top of her head. "Fiona helped me to find the courage to see that, to stop running away from it." He smiled. "It was a gift."

He turned to run his hands over Willie's ears. "Now we have to help Amy to stop running away from her diabetes."

Grace looked up at him quickly in time to see the brightness of his eyes. "Last night," he said, "I told her I'd give the world and anything I've ever had if she didn't have diabetes," he said.

For a moment they didn't say anything.

Then her father spoke again. "I told her to be brave. Everyday brave. And that's the hardest kind of courage there is. I told her to stay on her diet and take her insulin. I told her we love her and that someday someone is going to come along with a cure for diabetes."

He stood up. "And that's the day I'm waiting for."

Grace patted Willie's bony back, then she stood up too.

Her father smiled. "There's more to the message from Amy. She said to tell you she's going to try to stay on her diet. She said she loves you. And" he started to

laugh—"she said you're a big brat for saying what you did to her."

Grace began to laugh too. Then after a moment she buried her head in her father's chest and began to cry. They stood there for a long time, her father patting the back of her head until finally she pulled away. "I'll be late for school," she said.

Back in the kitchen she ate her breakfast standing at the counter. Then she went upstairs to get dressed.

Fifteen minutes later she turned the corner at Front Street and headed for school. She couldn't get the words she had said to Amy out of her mind. *"Why don't you do what you're supposed to do?"*

Suddenly she thought of Fiona. Yesterday afternoon. Fiona running around the yard, thinking Buddy was dangerous. Trying to save Willie. Afraid.

She stood still, holding a clump of snow in her hand. It was cold and hard. She remembered the Pirate Queen and the men in front of the post office. She could never be brave like that.

She didn't have to be. She didn't even have to be as brave as Amy. Everyday brave.

All she had to do was go up to Mrs. Raphael's desk. All she had to do was to say, "I broke your bell. I'm sorry."

Mrs. Raphael wouldn't like her as much anymore. She wouldn't call on her to go on messages. Maybe she'd even send her to the principal.

But that's what she had to do.

She dropped the clump of snow. Her hands were stinging. Then she went quickly across the school yard to wait until Mike opened the doors.

21

"Forget your homework again?" Mike asked as he opened the heavy doors.

Grace shook her head. Her mouth was so dry that it felt as if she couldn't move her tongue. "My teacher," she said finally as she walked around him and went up the stairs. "I have to tell my teacher something."

"She's not up there yet," Mike called after her.

Grace didn't turn around. She climbed the rest of the stairs and went down the corridor to stand at the classroom door and wait.

A few minutes later she heard Mrs. Raphael's footsteps on the stairs.

She pressed her hands tightly against the sides of her jeans. Think of the Pirate Queen, she told herself. The men at the post office, Amy.

She watched Mrs. Raphael start down the corridor

toward her, watched the little line appear between her eyebrows when she saw Grace waiting for her.

"What are you doing here, Grace?" she asked. "You know you're not supposed to—"

"I have to . . . have to tell you something."

"It won't wait until the bell rings?"

Grace shook her head. "Please."

Mrs. Raphael stopped at the door and fished around in her pocketbook for her keys. "All right." She opened the door and walked into the room ahead of Grace. "Come on then. Come in."

Grace leaned against the door. Then she straightened up.

"What is it, Grace?" Mrs. Raphael said irritably from across the room. She set her pocketbook down on her desk, picked up the big black plan book, and began to turn the pages.

Grace took a deep breath. "I broke your bell," she said.

Mrs. Raphael looked up sharply. "It's right here on my desk."

"Not that one. That's not the same one."

Slowly Mrs. Raphael closed the plan book and put it back on her desk. "Not the same one?" She reached out and picked up the bell.

Grace shook her head. "I bought that one at the big mall. In Binghamton." She ran her tongue over the edge of her lip.

Mrs. Raphael set the bell back on the desk. "What are you talking about, Grace? Speak up. The bell's right here."

"I came up after school last Friday. I came back for my social studies book. I picked up the bell. I just wanted to take a look at it. I thought it was so beautiful." She held her hands out, palms up. "I broke it."

Mrs. Raphael blinked and pushed the hair off the back of her neck. "But . . ."

"Lisa told me where I could buy another one."

"So," Mrs. Raphael said, "Lisa was involved in this. I knew it."

"No. She just told me that she had seen one in the Binghamton mall. She didn't know . . ." Grace shook her head. "I wanted her to have something to give you. I didn't know she had already—"

"Come here," Mrs. Raphael said.

Slowly Grace walked over to the desk.

"Now," Mrs. Raphael said. "Am I to understand that you came up here, picked up the bell, and dropped it?"

"I'm sorry."

Mrs. Raphael touched one of the angel's wings. "I remember when they gave it to me. I was a new teacher. I loved it because it reminded me of a happy time."

Grace could see the sadness in her eyes. Mrs. Raphael blinked again. "Why didn't you tell me?"

Grace looked down at the books she was carrying in her arms. Then she looked up and blurted out, "I was afraid."

Mrs. Raphael pushed her chair back. "Afraid? Afraid of what?"

Grace raised her shoulders a little.

"Afraid of me," Mrs. Raphael said. "Oh, Grace, how terrible." She put her plan book down.

"I know."

"No." Mrs. Raphael waved her hand impatiently. "It's terrible that children are afraid of me. I will have to think about that."

She stood up. "If you had told me the truth . . . I thought someone had taken it. I thought Lisa had . . . I blamed her."

Mrs. Raphael sighed. "Breaking the bell wasn't such a terrible thing. What was wrong was not telling me even though it would have been hard." Mrs. Raphael tightened her mouth. "Sometimes we have to do hard things in life. It was hard for me to leave my other school."

"Then why . . ." Grace began.

"Times change," Mrs. Raphael said. "The school closed. There weren't enough children in Warwick. . . ." She shook her head. "But to think that children are afraid of me now." She looked down at the bell. "The important thing about the bell was the memory. I still have that. It's up here." She touched her forehead. "I have that forever."

Grace cleared her throat. "I made you a card."

Mrs. Raphael nodded absently.

"I wanted it to be special. I didn't have . . ."

Mrs. Raphael looked up at her carefully. "You didn't have any money left after the bell. Is that it?"

Grace nodded. "The card isn't so good. I couldn't get it the way I wanted it."

"I didn't see it," Mrs. Raphael said.

"It's there, under someone's present."

"I'll find it," she said, "and I'll save it. It really is a special card, Grace. It will make me remember this Christmas."

Suddenly there was noise. Voices and clattering feet. "Lisa," Mrs. Raphael said. "I owe that child an apology. And you do too."

Grace nodded. "I know," she said. She turned and saw the children coming into the room. Mrs. Raphael looked up at her. "All right," she said. "You may go to your seat."

Grace hung her coat up in the closet, said hello to Bianca, then sat down at her desk. She still felt shaky but her mouth wasn't as dry. Mrs. Raphael was right. She had to tell Lisa.

She looked across the aisle. Lisa had tucked her hat in her desk so that the purple pompom was sticking out. She was pulling at the strands of wool and humming to herself.

Andrew had already started to hitch his desk away from her. Edward would be next.

Grace pulled a sheet of paper out of her notebook and leaned over it. *Dear Lisa,* she began. *I have to tell you . . .*

She looked at it for a moment, then she crumpled it up and stuck it in her desk.

In front of the room Mrs. Raphael was writing spelling words on the blackboard. They were all about Christmas. *Holiday . . . spirit . . . present.*

She still didn't have a present for Fiona.

She copied the spelling words, wrote them three times each, then began to do the rest of the boardwork. She didn't look up until she heard Mrs. Raphael tapping on the desk.

"Recess," Mrs. Raphael said. "It will have to be indoors. It's too cold and snowy to go outside today."

In the gym Grace watched as Mrs. Raphael called Lisa over to her. She whispered to Lisa for a few minutes. Lisa nodded, then she went over to the edge of the gym and started to bounce a ball.

The boys were playing tag and most of the girls were at the volleyball net.

"Come on," Bianca yelled to Grace. "We need more kids."

Grace shook her head and edged her way around the

gym. As she got closer to Lisa, she could hear her mumbling in time with the ball: "*C* my name is Carol and my husband's name is . . ." She bounced the ball an extra time. "Catherine."

"Catherine?" Grace asked.

"Can't think of anything for a man."

"Carl?"

"I should have known that."

"Or . . ." Grace thought for a moment and shrugged. "I guess that's all."

Lisa began to bounce the ball again. "*D* . . ."

"It was me with the bell," Grace said.

Lisa stopped bouncing. "You?" The ball dribbled away from her. "How come?"

"I didn't mean to get you into trouble. Really. I broke the bell and then after I bought a new one at the mall . . ." She broke off and began again. "You said you didn't have a present for her."

Lisa dove after the ball. "I thought it was Andrew or somebody like that."

"No. It was me. I told Mrs. Raphael."

Lisa stood there, head down, for a moment. Then she nodded once. "It's okay."

Grace looked around, trying to think of something to say. "My goat, Willie, had babies last night."

Lisa's face lit up. "How many?"

"Two. Do you want to come over and see them?"

From the other side of the gym Andrew zigzagged

toward them. Edward was right behind him. They darted past Grace and Lisa.

"Come over your house?" Lisa asked in a loud voice. "Yeah. When?"

Grace could feel her face redden. Andrew had turned around to look at them. "Tomorrow."

Lisa nodded. "I will."

"Come on, Grace," Bianca yelled.

Grace looked at the volleyball net, then back at Lisa. "I'm going to play," she said.

A thick strand of hair covered one of Lisa's eyes. She pushed it back. "All right."

Grace stood there hesitating. "Do you want to play?" she asked finally.

Lisa pushed at her hair again. Then she shook her head.

Grace started across the gym alone. Halfway there she looked back. Lisa was bouncing the ball again. Feeling guilty, she began to run.

22

After dismissal Grace turned the corner of Front Street and headed across Mr. Hunt's field. The day was over. She took a deep breath. Over.

Ralph, Mr. Hunt's goat, was standing at the chicken wire, chewing on a stick.

"Hey, Ralphie," she yelled. "Willie had babies."

She started to run. She couldn't wait to get home to see Fiona. She didn't even stop when she reached Willie's pen. She'd go out and give her something to eat and look at the babies in a few minutes. But first she wanted to tell Fiona something.

Fiona wasn't in the kitchen.

"Fiona?" Grace yelled. "Where are you?"

She raced upstairs. But even before she called out, she could tell no one was there. It was so quiet in her

bedroom that she could hear the soft hum of the refrigerator downstairs in the kitchen.

Maybe Fiona was gone. Maybe she had gone back
to Ireland. Maybe . . .

Suppose she never saw Fiona again. Fiona smiling.
Singing. She whirled around and ran downstairs. Maybe
she was outside. She went to the back door and pulled
it open. "Fiona," she yelled. "Please, Fiona. Where are
you?"

Her clothes. If she had gone, she would have taken
. . . She rushed back into Fiona's room and yanked
the closet door open.

They were still there, all of Fiona's things, hanging in
a neat row. She reached for the Aran sweater Fiona
wore sometimes and held the wool against her cheek.
Maybe Fiona was at the hospital. Maybe Amy was
worse.

Then she heard the back door slam. "Grania," a
voice called.

Grace didn't stop to close the closet door. She ran
into the kitchen. "I was looking for you. I thought you
were gone."

"I was way out in back," Fiona said. "I went into the
fields behind Mr. Hunt's house."

"Don't go back to Ireland," Grace said. "Don't ever
go back."

Fiona smiled and reached out for her with both
hands. "I told your father I'd never stay unless you

asked me." She hugged Grace to her. "And I said I'd never leave as long as you wanted me here."

Grace threw her arms around Fiona's thick waist. "I want you," she whispered. After a moment she stepped back. "Where were you?"

Fiona took a breath. "That devil dog," she said. "I was making a pudding, I was, when I saw that great thing up on the porch. At first I wanted to take the broom to him. . . ."

"Oh, no, Fiona. Not to Buddy."

"That's right, me girl. I said to myself that I had to stir up my courage because you loved that monster of a dog and that maybe I'd let him in the house. He'd be here waiting for you when you came home from school." Fiona nodded grimly. "So I opened the door a crack to see if he wanted to come in."

"And . . ."

"And he wagged his tail at me and ran into the yard. And I after him, trying to get him to come in." Fiona threw her arms up in the air. "Whoosh. Every time I took a step he took four and the next thing you know we were both up in the woods. I finally gave up."

"He thought you were playing. He'll be back," Grace said. She thought for a moment. "That took a lot of courage."

Fiona sat down across from her. "Well, me girl, you've taught me courage. I told Katie, your mother, years ago, that I'd never go near a dog again."

Grace shook her head. "That's what I want to tell you, Fiona. I don't know why you keep thinking I'm brave. I'm not. I did a terrible thing because I was afraid."

"Oh, Grania, everyone's afraid sometimes," Fiona said. "Courage is a gift and we can't expect to have it with us always." She stood very still. "Do you want to tell me about it."

Grace nodded. She leaned against the kitchen counter and began to tell Fiona the story.

Fiona shook her head and clucked softly but she didn't say a word until Grace was finished.

"Your mother . . ." Fiona said then. She broke off and began again. "There's something I wanted to give you. I was going to wrap it up with your other Christmas presents, but I think I'll give it to you now." She turned and went toward her bedroom. "It's nice to get a Christmas present early once in a while," she said over her shoulder.

Grace felt her face redden. What would she do about Fiona's present?

"Come on," Fiona said.

Grace followed her into the bedroom and watched as Fiona dragged her suitcase out from under the bed.

"It's the only thing left inside," Fiona said. She pulled out a flat package wrapped in tissue paper. Then she sat down on the edge of the bed and patted the spread. "Sit here with me." She looked around. "It would be nice if we could find a chair for in here," she said, handing Grace the package.

"There's one in the garage," Grace said. "A green one."

She slipped her finger under the tape on the package. Inside was a photograph of two girls. One of them was sitting on a horse, the other was standing next to her. It was easy to see that the girl on the horse was Fiona. Even then one of Fiona's eyes was staring straight ahead and the other was tilted out just the tiniest bit.

"There I am on my neighbor's horse," Fiona said, pointing. She touched the picture gently. "How I loved that horse."

"I thought you didn't like animals."

"Dogs," Fiona said. "Only dogs. But horses? There isn't an Irishman anywhere who doesn't love horses." She pointed to the other girl in the picture. "And there's Katie, your mother, next to me."

Grace looked at the picture curiously. Her mother, small and thin, and looking like Amy, stared back at her seriously.

"I've had the picture all these years," Fiona said, "to remind me of that awful dog on Tanner's Lane and the Pirate Queen and . . ." Fiona smiled. "I was going to say your mother. But I don't need a picture for that. I can see her just as clearly . . ." Fiona closed her eyes for a second. "Just before the man came around to take this picture, my mother sent me for something on Tan-

ner's Lane. I met Katie on the way. We knew each
other, of course, but we weren't friends yet."

Fiona tapped the picture with her finger. "Anyway,
Katie walked along with me. I was glad because I was
afraid of the dog that lived on Tanner's Lane. He was
always straining at his chain. Big, he was, with his
teeth always bared."

Grace nodded and looked again at the picture of her
mother, trying to remember her.

"That day the dog got loose. He came after us, he
did, and cornered me near the fence. 'Run, Katie,' I
yelled, and she did. She climbed the fence and hid
behind a tree. And the dog came after me."

"Did he hurt you?"

"I have the scar on my leg still, like a little circle."

"But how did you get away?"

"Katie, your mother," Fiona said. "Suddenly she
came running back, yelling like a banshee, waving
her arms." Fiona nodded. "Like a banshee," she said
again softly.

Grace looked at the picture. "Then what?"

Fiona smiled. "Then the dog backed off and his owner
came out and chained him up. Katie put her arms
around me and said she'd never run away again. And
from then on we were friends, Katie and I."

They sat there quietly for a few minutes, then Grace
realized she could see her mother's face, not blurry the
way it usually was, but sharp and clear. Her mother

finding the gift of courage and running after the dog, her mother casting her line into the water on a sunny day, her mother smiling at her.

Suddenly Lisa popped into her mind. Lisa, dirty and loud. She thought back to what Bianca had said about Lisa not caring. And then she remembered Lisa running for the candy, grabbing the notebook.

They had been wrong about Lisa, she was sure. There were a lot of things Lisa cared about. She thought about Lisa bringing the present for Mrs. Raphael wrapped in yellow paper. And Lisa loving her goat Willie.

It would be hard to be Lisa's friend. Everyone else . . . She shook her head. She'd have to try. Wait till Lisa saw Willie's babies. Maybe when the babies grew a little, she'd think of giving her one. She'd have to see.

"Come now," Fiona said, "and I'll start the supper. After we eat, the doctor said you can see Amy for a minute or two."

Grace looked up. "Is she all right?"

Fiona nodded. "I was there this morning. She's fine. Almost ready to come home."

"I'll bring the picture to show her," Grace said. She started for the kitchen behind Fiona. "You didn't tell me. What was the horse's name?"

Fiona stopped and thought for a moment. "Star, it was," she said. "Star."

Grace smiled at her. She knew what she'd give Fiona for Christmas. The horse pictures up in her closet. She'd take them out and put some mounting paper around them. Fiona would love them. Molly, and Big Tom, and Star, up on the wall in the back bedroom again. Right where they belonged.

About the Author

===========

Patricia Reilly Giff is the author of *Have You Seen Hyacinth Macaw?*, a mystery, and the popular books about Casey Valentine and her friends—*Fourth-Grade Celebrity, The Girl Who Knew It All, Left-Handed Shortstop* (available in Dell Yearling editions), and *The Winter Worm Business*. She divides her time between Elmont and Harvard, New York.